ELEMENTAL

A SHORT STORY ANTHOLOGY

Breakthrough Book Collective

First published in Great Britain in 2024 by Breakthrough Books.

www.breakthroughbookcollective.com

Print ISBN: 978-1-0687185-0-2

CONTENTS

'And new Philosophy calls all in doubt, the element of fire is quite put out; the Sun is lost, and the earth, and no man's wit can well direct him where to look for it.'

-JOHN DONNE

A DAY FOR ALL SEASONS

MARK BOWSHER

Today's the day – the universe willed it into being and now it is here. A day for all seasons.

It begins with winter. Of course it does. First, we must crack through the shell of dark to find the light. We all are shivering, shaking heaps; stiff and cocooned in blankets in this grey corner of the year. Humanity locked away from one another, trapped alone with all the horrors of our unforgiving minds, until spring's merciful release invites us out to play.

But the curse of our tormented solitude slithers away as the sun sulks heavily over the horizon, instilled with all the cold dread of a Monday in January. We are reluctant to venture out on this bitter morning. Home never feels more homely than it does in winter.

In time, we emerge for our single night hibernation. The dim light is kind to our waking eyes, though offers no warmth to our souls. The sun shelters behind a mottled sky. All the despairs of life and the death to come creeps about us, weighs us down, hunches us forward. We stare at our feet as we trudge through the snow.

The crisp crack of the frozen rain crunches under foot, satisfying, a flicker of a smile, it lingers, brightness in the pure white ground. Lighter and lighter the snow becomes as the sun banishes the clouds.

Now, as the sun arches high into the sky, nearing midday – reminding us that winter's curse has hidden the world in shadow for too much of the day – the land becomes bright.

A crisp blue winter sky. The world lit by snow. Daydreams of arctic landscapes, vast mountains and glaciers. As we enter the park and see children and adults alike wrapped up warm against the cruel cold. Face-achingly broad smiles as they pelt each other with snowballs. Nothing beats a clear day in winter.

Unless spring arrives. Yes, spring is always waiting to burst forth from under the tyranny of winter's frosted grip. Snow melts away, ice, sludge, and then nothing. The firm ground softens. The daffodils and snowdrops push upward through the soil. Everything becomes fresh and green. No season gives more of a feeling of hope than spring.

Those who remained inside during winter's elongated reign, emerge, blinking. The world is alive again. Most of the day is spring – not yet blisteringly hot nor still chill down to the aching bones.

Now is the time to venture into the woods, see life, hear the birds and creatures of the woods. Singing and scurrying and snapping of twigs. Paddling in rivers and brooks and readying ourselves for the stifling summer when we replace wading in streams with diving into the rushing waves of the sea. The sun is warm yet gentle, forgiving.

Spring stretches on, all the way until the slow dive of the sun.

Now, in the day's most gleeful plot twist, we skip a season. It is the perfect time for autumn. The temperature remains constant, simply a spring climate with a hint of bitterness foreshadowing the winter to come hidden in the breeze. The leaves blaze orange and yellow with the sun, brown, curl, and fly off with the wind. The airborne stream of dried leaves twists and turns, caught in the amber glow of the sleepy star.

Collapsing in a bed of leaves in the park, the whistling wind all around us, a deep orange glow lighting the world. This is the best and most glorious marriage of time of day and season to be seen in the entire year.

Then, against all the odds, the day turns back. As it draws to a close, the day stretches on, overindulging in its own finale, rewarding those robbed of light in winter's morning by bringing on summer's dusk.

Here, at long last, the season we've all been waiting for, sneaking in before the day's close.

The air is stuffed with heat, the sun appears to pedal backwards through the sky, its hue changing from deep orange to amber then pale egg yolk yellow in an ocean blue sky. Splodges of yellow with blue tails dance before our eyes as we reel from the sun's glare.

Summer's sun is in no rush to set. Tables are brought from houses, parties with cake and lemonade and bubbling, intoxicating mixtures, and there is music and dancing and grass is turned to hay and the day goes on and on. The old lie goes 'time flies when you're enjoying yourself' but the day feels longer than it is here and now – when there is merriment to be had, time stretches on and on and joyously on.

As we sit on the hill overlooking over the city, the sun dips contentedly into the horizon and the summer stars come out to shine. Summer's night is as warm as spring's brightest day.

Summer may be nothing more than a few hours long, yet it is the same sun which rears its glorious head in each month, burning away the clouds. Right now, as summer warms us, we lie on the grass, sweating, comfortably glowing within and without, dreaming of that perfect, crisp winter day, plunging into the pure white snow, its invigorating coolness awakening us from the sting of heat in summer's open-eyed slumber.

We stretch out our arms and legs, feeling the curve of the earth. The planet turns, the stars spin in the sky, but we remain the singular stationary point in this relentless universe. We are dizzy with delight and lost in the thankless eternity. Time has twisted and turned today, bending reality completely out of shape. All the wonders of a year condensed into a day flit through our mind and we are weighed down by the grief of all those passings in the last 365 turns of the Earth.

We breathe in deep, fill our lungs to breaking point and stow away all that pain in our pocket for another day. We will deal with all the horrors of life soon – smash it, forgive it, eat it whole, as we wish – but we will not be dragged to the bottom of the deepest, coldest ocean on this one perfect day.

We close our eyes and are warm, ready for whatever tomorrow may throw our way.

BREATHE IN THE WATER

PENNY PEPPER

They don't talk about the barnacles in the books. They crust on my aged tail, like the corns my old Nana used to have on the Dry. Nana, the only human I loved. My hair is no longer a fable. Not the wild plethora of old, not a luscious siren whirl around me. It is strings and tattered weed and it tangles at the slightest turn.

When I first came here, it was raw and unexpected. It took me a while to adjust, but then Finn found me. Scooped me up, pulled me into his strong arms and cocooned me in his own ebullient locks that moved with the tides, issuing seahorses and sea-snails from the twists when he shook with laughter.

I recall my first Sea day. A death of one kind and a birth of another. The cliffs were not so high but sufficient for the closure I craved. Many times I walked to that place, away from the horrors of that tiny square box they call home. They say home is where you belong, but I did not fit in that space of constraints and rules. Those who claimed to love me did so for their own ambiguous needs – needs obscure and unspoken. I languished in a place that is much colder than the threat of any waves that may freeze you.

The journey was long and painful. Long in terms of effort, and the time it took, rather than the distance. But my last day on the Dry was beautiful, a melting sky of orange and pink. As I drew my last Dry breath I wondered for a second if I would miss flowers of those colours but sensed that hidden in the ocean I would find equivalence.

Those of the Sea have haunted those of the Dry. In the deepest places some say that we are entwined in our histories and our mythologies – and that is how we were born. We are creatures of curiosity, but we are curious in ourselves and sometimes we yearn to try that life – for some the ache is to return to it. As I paused on the cliff, bathed in the colours of the sinking sun, I looked for nothing but release and knew in my deepest gut I would not be missed. Beyond that, no thought held me back. Not my mother, with her moods and disappointments. Not my one brother, who fled the lie of home as soon as he was able. And never my father, with his hard, cursing hand and words of blame sharp throughout my childhood. Family could do nothing but create me as a creature glacial with fear and spirals of illness both inexplicable and constant.

Later, when I followed the Giants, the gods of our Sea, down to the south, how I was taught to play! My hair grew and grew, my skin scaled up where it needed to, and I learned to ride those Giants with respect, and only upon invitation. What then, of that strange square box once called home? Now my home was without boundary as I breathed in the water, found new mothers, fathers and playmates, living and loving in a happy abyss of wonder and inquisitiveness I had not known lived within me.

But when I took the step I did not hate myself and even now I wonder, did I hesitate? Did the cliff falter, crumbling as I moved? Did the earth itself push me into my new life?

How cold it was, the unspeakable shock. The urge to fight was strong though I didn't break at once, as I'd expected, but bobbed and rolled and argued with the Sea. But then, I let go. I breathed in the taste of salt and dragged that cold surging element into my lungs. I felt water possess me and ravish my lonely, young bones.

Yet there came the sound of lightest gurgled laughter and a woman of the water lifted me up and stroked my hair. Hair that was short and practical, though once it was long. Back when Nana would comb it and say it was beautiful. The sea woman lifted me high and I gazed in wonder at her eyes, never once afraid or caught in judgement as to our differences. And soon she sang, a low, rolling lullaby as she carried me in her arms, discarding my clothes gently as we moved with the flow of the tides and deeper into the darkening blue. For once, the darkness did not bring fear but respite. And soon there were others, soothing me with their own songs, with gifts of glowing fish and luminescent shells. As I evolved to become a creature of the Sea, the rules of the Dry fell away. Now there was no time but seasons and the changing face of the moon. And I was reborn when it shone at its fullest across the gentle waters.

Finn had come from the Dry, too, finding me fifteen bright moons beyond my rebirth. His story was as sorrowful as mine, when his father took him in his wheelchair to the dock on a night so dark even the eyes of owls couldn't judge him. As they neared the black water, his father soothed him, sang a soft song and spun words about easing pain and suffering as he tipped his son into the deep. The father walked away from his son's cries, his desperate splashes, and gave him away as easily as a stone dropped casually into the depths.

The waves loved Finn and carried him to new parents. They caught hold of his weak legs, grasped him and shook their sleek heads in shame at what the Dry folk do to those they deem different.

As was I, in my own way. Emotions out on my skin, raw from my eyes, bleeding fear and joy from my heart in equal measure. I did not belong with the dull every day on the Dry and it was in the Sea that I found my home. To love and live for many moons and many seasons. To travel, replete with love for Finn.

It is said by the elders and the whales that when we die we melt into the Sea. We become it, it becomes us and as long as there are seas and planets and stars – and lost folk who want to believe in the extraordinary – we will prevail.

I breathe in the water and know Finn, gone since spring high-tides, is within me again. Our children swam far to find lovers of their own long ago and I know it is my time to rest in the waves, to smile as I dissolve, slow and soft, watched by red crabs and rainbow coral, into the essence of my love, my darling ocean love. Our two different troubled streams now one, loved and absorbed by the accepting Sea.

HERE COMES THE FLOOD

PETE LANGMAN

From high above, they looked like rivers slowly meandering towards the sea, rivers chased and harried by smaller tributaries intent on joining the main stream. But they seemed to be flowing backwards, inland and towards the mountains, gathering momentum as they approached the higher ground, larger streams shrinking as they came ever closer to an as-yet invisible source.

Noel stood on the side of the mountain and surveyed the plains below, his left hand shielding his eyes from the relentless desert sun. The labyrinthine weave of motion may have resembled the return of the waters of the sea towards the highlands of their genesis, but looks, as Noel well knew, were all too often deceptive. In any case, he also knew the destination sought by these dark streams. It stood directly behind him.

Not for the first time Noel thought about the hoary old saying 'ignorance is bliss', and how it had more than a whiff of wisdom about it. It was knowledge that made the sight so terrifying. And then there was the noise. Oh, the noise. It flowed up the mountainside to lap at his ears like evening ripples caressing the shores of a lake in autumn, but as it leaked out of the plains below the volume seemed to grow rather than subside as it ought.

Noel was hardly an ingenue. After all, he'd only recently celebrated his six hundred and thirty-seventh birthday. There wasn't much that he hadn't seen at first hand. But even Noel had struggled to imagine quite how this moment would feel. Now, with every passing minute, his imagination appeared increasingly inadequate. Reality had already outpaced him, which rather suggested that the immediate future didn't bear thinking about. He simply stared at the darkness gathering on the horizon like a stain. Then at the scroll that he held in his right hand.

'You sure we've read this right?' he said.

'Sorry Dad, what did you say?' The voice was slightly muffled by the scarf that was wrapped around its owner's face. There was a thud as two heavily booted feet hit the dry, stony earth. The young man connected to them walked over to where Noel stood.

'I said, are you sure we've read this right, Shiv?' He looked at his son, his sunburnt face, hands rough from hard manual labour, the folds of his clothes clogged up with sawdust and fine, red sand. 'I mean, I look at this, look at that, and then... that, and it seems to me there's been some sort of error.' Noel waved the scroll in his son's face, gestured at the huge construction project taking shape behind him, and then at the darkness that appeared to be spreading over the land beneath them. 'I think we're going to need a bigger boat.'

'What do you...' Shiv's voice tailed off and was swallowed up by the tidal flow of ambient noise that was now up to their ankles. He coughed as a sudden whip-tail of gritty wind reached into his open mouth and plucked the moisture from it. 'Jeez... dad, that's one hell of a storm that's brewing...'

'That's not...' said Noel, as he saw his son grab a can of beer from the eski. Shiv cracked it open and took a long draught. He exhaled a sigh of highly localised contentment and then took the scroll from his father's hand. 'Well,' he said, scanning the length of papyrus. 'These are the only instructions we have.'

'Yes,' said his father. 'That's all we have. I'm just wondering whether we've read them right.'

'Followed them to the letter,' said Shiv. 'There isn't another translation, is there?'

'Translation?' Noel looked at his son.

'You know, dad, like with those flatpack projects. The 'build your shed with just a hammer and adze' boxes. They usually come with lots of versions in different languages. Maybe the translator was having a bad day – if there was another one we could compare the two for accuracy'.

'Shiv. It's in the one, universal language,' said Noel. 'An early version, to be sure, but universal nonetheless.'

'Ok,' said Shiv. 'But look. We followed the instructions to the letter, dad, as I said. While you were,' at this Shiv looked a little sheepish. 'Resting.' Noel looked at his son disapprovingly. 'We have built this boat to plan, as accurately as we know how. If it's not a translation issue it must be something else. We followed the plan. You're not going to tell me that the plan is wrong, are you? I mean, that really isn't an avenue we ought to be going down right now, if you get my meaning.'

'But Shiv. Does that look like 300 cubits to you, son?' said Noel, shaking his head in exasperation. 'What do I always say?'

'Yeah, yeah... Measure once, cut twice,' said Shiv, muttering something else indistinctly under his breath.

'No, idiot,' said Noel, approaching apoplexy. 'Measure twice, cut once.' He stared at his son once more.

'I know, dad.' Shiv paused, for effect. 'We all know. I'd be surprised if your ass didn't know, you say it often enough. 'Zacc measured everything very, very carefully.'

At this, Noel's arms dropped to his sides and the scroll fell from his hand. 'Shiv,' he said, his voice taking on the quiet, low tones his son had long recognised as indicating the onset of a suitably patriarchal rage. 'Shiv, my dear, dear boy. Zacc is a dwarf.' Noel turned around, surveyed the ark in all its rather truncated glory, and sighed.

Shiv looked sheepish. 'I did wonder why we had so much gopherwood left over. I thought you'd maybe ordered after a beer too many...'

'For the love of...' started Noel, though thought better of it. Now was definitely not the time to be alerting HIM to any last-minute hitches.

'We've got the wood, let's build another!' said Shiv, triumphant.

Noel just stared at him. 'This one took us forty days.'

'So we can work nights and build another in twenty,' said Shiv. 'Probably quicker, seeing as we know how it fits together now, and most of the wood has already been cut to size. We could rationalise the superstructure to save another day or two...'

'What do you mean?'

'Well,' said Shiv. 'Get some decent tarps instead of fully roofing it.'

'No, not that part,' his father said, interrupting him. 'The part about having the wood already cut to size.'

'When we first measured up we found that most of the timbers were double the length needed so we ... oh.'

'Oh, indeed,' said Noel. 'You'll be telling me next that you only got through half the nails and half of the pitch too. But it's all rather academic now, in any case.' At this he raised his arm and directed Shiv's gaze to the ever-darkening horizon, before himself looking to the heavens as the first drops of rain fell indolently onto the desert floor, kicking up little clouds of dust that were immediately slapped back down to earth by a second wave of drops. Shiv looked in the direction indicated.

'Dad,' he said. 'Those clouds. The big, black ones on the horizon. They're not actually a storm, are they? They're our, er, passengers, aren't they?'

'Well, of a sort, yes,' said Noel. 'All of animal kind. Heading our way.'

'That... they... us? Fuck,' said Shiv. 'You're right, we are going to need a bigger boat.'

The two men fell silent for a few moments as the true scale of the task ahead began to sink in. Shiv rarely listened to his father. Perhaps it was an inherited characteristic. When Noel had accepted this contract he had been warned that HE was especially poor at giving estimates. Right from 'The Beginning', when there was meant just to be The Word, HE had insisted on changing the specifications at the last minute. First there was The Word, then it was God, then it was with God... and it's all very well saying 'let there be Light', but it's really important to explain exactly what this 'Light' was. HE expected it simply to 'Be.'

No matter how hard the contractors explained that yes, the idea of uncovering the face of the deep was all well and good in principle, but at some point someone needs to specify exactly what a 'deep' was so that you could uncover its 'face' with your 'light', HE was having none if it. And then there was the schedule. Let's just say that the overtime stretched a fair way beyond the seventh day, and they were still fiddling about with some of the mechanisms now. The unions were not happy, and then HE had complained that his pets hadn't come out quite as he'd hoped so now he was going to drown them all and start again. Which had the liberals up in arms, and anyway, it wasn't as if it could all be done with a snap of his fingers. Noel knew all this, but still took the job. It would be a way of cementing his reputation, ensuring the firm's viability over the coming millennia. He really couldn't say no, though now he was rather wishing he had.

'Dad,' said Shiv. 'Dad!'

'Sorry, son,' said Noel. 'I was just...'

'Having a senior moment, I know.'

'Cheeky sod,' said Noel. 'You wait 'til you're six hundred and something, then you can laugh about it.' He shook his head, muttering.

'I've got an idea,' said Shiv.

Noel stared at his son, expectantly. Silence. 'Well come on, don't keep it to yourself,' he said, flicking the brim of his hat to release some of the water that was gathering to make a grand entrance between the collar of his shirt and his neck. 'We haven't got all day!'

'We control what we can control,' said Shiv.

'What does that mean?' asked Noel.

'Exactly,' said Shiv, smiling. 'We know HE can be a bit of a micro manager but so long as we have the paperwork we can be more judicious in our passenger selection criteria.'

'Uh-huh,' said Noel, not having a clue what his son was talking about but happy to consider any way out of this mess.

'We look at who's expecting a ride? Do they have tickets? Do they have legal representation?'

'Pardon?'

'We cut down the numbers through judicious application of obtuse bureaucracy. What does the book say, anyway?'

'Oh,' said Noel. 'Something about the animals.'

'How many of them?'

'All of them,' said Noel.

'All of... them?' said Shiv, looking at the massed ranks of fauna assembling below their vantage point. 'There are enough there to fill a hundred of these arks, even if we had made them full size.'

'HE never was much for careful calculation,' said Noel. 'The bloody scroll's already full of stuff that doesn't add up, and from what I hear the sequel's even more confusing, and as for the season finale...'

'Oh,' said Shiv. 'That the one full of trumpets and vials and seven thises and seven thats and not even HE knows what else?'

'That's the one,' said Noel. 'But the contract specifically states two pairs of unclean animals, seven pairs of clean ones.'

'And we know which is which, how?'

'Oh, it's all explained later on in the scroll,' said Noel. 'Or, at least, it will be when HE has got round to writing it. I think it's this *nunc stans* business.

I suppose that when you live in the eternal present, there's no such thing as late. Or early, come to that matter. So deadlines don't really make any sense.'

'Great,' said Shiv. 'I knew there'd be a neat get-out clause.'

'Go on...' said Noel.

'Well, we can decide which animals are clean and which unclean,' said Shiv. 'If we go vegan, all animals are unclean, so we can just take them in two-by-two.'

'I doubt we'll need to worry about that,' said Noel. 'After a few hours on the ark there won't be a clean beast on the boat.'

'There you go,' said Shiv. 'And just take two of every type.'

'It says two pairs,' said Noel. 'HE won't be happy.'

'Oh do grow yourself a pair ... hang on,' said Shiv. 'There you go. Each animal is going to have a pair of something. That'll do.' He paused. 'Right, where have we got to?'

'By my maths, we've reduced the number of passengers by a factor of eighteen.'

'Perfect,' said Shiv.

'We'll get complaints.'

'Troublemakers don't get to come in,' said Shiv. 'They'll not argue with the Scroll.'

'It'd be easier if Adam were still around,' said Noel. 'He was quite the guy when it came to dealing with animals. Knew 'em all by their nature. Amazing.'

'Did he leave a list?' Shiv was smiling now. 'I mean, if your name's not on the list... this ark's only for the A-listers. If Adam gave them a name, they're in. Otherwise... and perhaps we should consider reputation management going forward.'

'What?'

'Consider how this will impact on the firm. 'This is all a big PR exercise, right? So we concentrate on stuff that's soundbite-friendly. You know, big picture stuff. Think of it as a legacy project. We can massage the guest-list so that the facts actually fit into a nursery rhyme. Future generations of children will sing songs about us, be taught about us in school, and it won't cost us a penny.'

'That's all well and good,' said Noel, 'but there'll still be enough qualifying animals left to fill a hundred arks.'

'So, we pick the good-looking ones. The useful ones. We have to be pragmatic.' With that, Noel's son finished his can and threw it onto the ground.

'Pick that up and put it in the recycling, oaf,' said Noel.

'Why bother?' replied his son. 'It's not like they'll be collecting next Monday, is it?'

'It's the principle,' said Noel. He stared at his son until he picked up the offending item, flattened it, and placed it in the appropriate receptacle.

'That's given me another idea!' said Shiv. 'We make a list of ones that look likely to get eaten and say they never survived the trip.'

'That's better,' said Noel. 'Now, let's look at these criteria.'

As they spoke, the darkness on the horizon continued to spread. And the tidal surge of noise grew ever more insistent. A cacophony of calls, roars, neighs, squeaks, gurgles, trumpets, bellows, brays, cackles, panthoots, buzzes and clicks flowed up towards Noel.

'Ok. So. Who do we leave behind?'

'It's pretty simple, dad,' said Shiv. 'We think of volume first. We can manage four cubic cubits of insect life. That's a few million pairs. We can fit perches on the outside for all the birds, nets for all the crustacea, we ignore the fish, the whales and dolphins and all that lot. We take some marquee mammals, and a few of the weirdos to keep our descendants guessing, and most of all, refuse entry to any of the really big ones and we're there. No-one's going to count. So long as we deliver "one Ark, full of animals" we're sorted.'

'Oh, it's that simple, is it? Remind me when this is all over and HE's having a fit that this was all your fault.'

'Oh, come on Dad, think about it,' said Shiv. 'No-one's going to miss the dinosaurs... they won't even notice they're gone.'

DESARÉ

ELENA KAUFMAN

The mythological figure, a Lilith-demon, features in ancient Mesopotamia and in Judaic literature. Both beautiful and lethal, she is a succubus who lures and seduces men to their deaths. All with her kiss.

We're happy, oh so happy. The couple you see hand-in-hand round the mini-market at sunset, that's us. He stops me beside the pineapples, clasps my chin in a muscular hand and kisses me, imprisons me. I stamp my lips on his until I leave my mark. Until the sun leaves a stain on the horizon. Until I stain him.

I am Desaré. To be desired. To be in disarray. Not to be erased.

A mermaid creature rising from velvety black water to embrace half-sleeping men. In this one's caged fantasy, I creep into his heart and head and take hold. Grasping with needy, nailed fingers. Entering his bloodstream. Peeling away secrets. Then lashing him with my tails.

I am Desaré and I make Adam's dreams come true. For a time.

He is 29 years old. I am older, so much older. As old as the seas. I can be as large as his fantasies, as small as his fingernail. A shapeshifter, a dreamy companion. He is single. I am too, for always. My status is unimportant. My sisters have fled, my parents – I have none. All gone. Community wrecked.

No fixed address. Nothing fixed. This is what I do. So many men, so many homes. So much to feed on. The basement of his parents' house is where this one lives. I will live with him, on him. It matters not where. But a home is what I need. A host. To feed from, to grow bigger. When I don't get sustenance, I shrink to the size of a tick, to nothing. I disappear.

What I enjoy most about Adam is his vitality and raunchy imagination. The basement is his man-cave and he thinks I am his slave. His parents do not know me, nor do I care to meet his mother. Danger, danger. For if I do, she will see through me. That will be the end. Adam is shy. All in good time, he says. I hide out, trust him. Like he trusts me.

Three months ago, I first found the boy-man submerged, as I was during a heatwave, one fateful night in an air-conditioned bar. I latched on to him at the counter. Discreetly. Did his friends even notice? At first, he observed me through droopy eyes, making the contact I needed to hook on. To stick in. His vision glazed, but his eyebrows raised. Stunned to see the woman he'd fantasised about standing there in front of him. You see, I'm the type to dream about. So many have, so many do. So many will. Wrapping his fingers in my long strands of hair until they are tangled like minnows in a net.

Adam is highly intelligent on paper. At work, he's well-dressed, well-liked. Commanding attention and respect while designing web apps. His mind knows no boundaries, endlessly fuelled by coffee, cocaine, energy drinks, video games, online porn. This man-boy has potential and I'm the type to dream about. So many have, so many do. So many will.

I am Desaré. To be desired. To be in disarray. Not to be erased.

His body is a delight to discover under cool silk sheets and feathered pillows. With deft hands, sharp and careful claws, I blow his mind, literally. For that's what I do: blow bodies, blow minds.

Adam merges into me and becomes even more reclusive, taking only every second dinner with his parents upstairs, cancelling weekend plans with friends and colleagues to hole up with his other half. Ailments riddle him. He bans his coddling mother from sending him to doctors, refuses to take medicines. His work suffers. He takes days off so we can stare eye-to-eye, sitting cross-legged on his comforter, bare knees touching. Since I have no one in my life, it is a delight that I am so needed and depended upon. I am in my element. Me in him and him in me.

Trays arrive at his bedroom door – stir-fried duck and chocolate cake, coffee, bottles of vitamins. His mother, the gourmet, dishes out tablets of magnesium, iron, vitamins D and C. Is his lack of energy from Covid or a tick bite? She wonders. He waves her away as if she were a fly, while I, the tick she imagines, gets all of him. And all of it he gives to me, feeding me with his fingers while starving himself. Generous Adam. I have done this before to other men. In other homes. With other mothers. Seeping under door frames or curling into corners. Expanding my large self. Contracting when needed.

It ends badly. Always does. I hurt them first. Sweet youth reared in privilege, served, and shaped to rule the world. To rule us. But we refuse. They cannot prise me off or decimate me. Hard to ignore someone who lives in your head. Someone who takes over your body, your faculties, eventually your thoughts, and then your vitals.

I am Desaré. To be in disarray.

This time, to my surprise, is different. What happens next mortifies me. A party for his birthday, a surprise. An intervention, more like. His jovial buddies resuscitating their friendship. A small group tramping to his basement door, demanding to see him by forcing a celebration. His 30th. Carting cases of beer, springing jokey gifts, trailing two lap dancers because I refuse to entertain. I tell him so.

'Go, then!' Adam demands, shoving me into the laundry room, clicking the lock. 'Don't come out!'

I shimmy out of a crack in the window and flee round the house to spy from their dark garden. What I witness through a side window turns me fiery with vengeance. Two strange women pawing at him, taking what is mine. A wild time is had by all, supposedly, and Adam forgets he has a girlfriend. A Lilith. Disrespects the gap I have shaped within him. Outside, on his lawn, I scratch my raspberry red nails along the window glass and leer at them, my mouth an angry slash.

He is the first man to hurt me, and I cannot let go of it. A month passes, and I cling on to him but I am losing energy, losing my grasp. I continue as if the party has had no effect. But he and I have run our course. Still, I try to burrow on like a juicy creature, but I am dry. One night, after he falls asleep, I wander in and out of pubs and come upon the perfect mate for my next round. This one is a wiser choice. Lives alone in a penthouse. Family-less. Makes immediate eye contact.

Safe to finish Adam off, then. I plan to drain him dry and leave a husk for his mother. Our night is reignited as if he has missed me, or only temporarily misplaced his love. His passion confuses me and I throw myself in, matching his impulse. But at the correct point to latch on, when I burrow in as I do, he pulls back and shakes me so hard it shatters my grip. With nimble fingers, he dangles me away from him and squeezes tighter and tighter. I shrink from the pressure, shrink and shrink until I fit into his fist. How had he known to do it? To turn me into a small creature by trapping me in his hand, silencing me. Adam shoves me into a glass jar. Turns the lid closed. Laughs till his eyes stream with tears.

Caught like a moth.

To be desired – no, to be erased.

To be in disarray. Desaré.

But no, not quite like that...

His glassy, giant eyes approach, his lips curl in a grin, while his fingers tap the glass to irritate. I rage, but my fury entertains him. He sets me on his shelf as a decoration. The next night, he has a party. Same guys, same girls. He holds the glass out, waving it in the air.

'My pet,' he says, with a leering smile. 'My little tick.' Spit splatters the glass and I cannot bear to look at those spoiled kids.

'You tricked me – you bitch.' He whispers with tense lips and shiny teeth.

In my glass prison, I wrap long strands of hair around my eyes, round and round, weaving a blanket of denial. A cocoon. The next day, his mother bustles in and I hear an argument. Hectic energy, rattling noises, so I unwrap my hair to see a hand descending onto my glass. Gold-ringed fingers, manicured nails. I shrink under her shadow as she grasps my glass. She throws me and I arc through the air, landing in a bin of beer bottles. Glass shatters.

Pieces fly and I hear her magnified voice as a shrill fury piercing the room. I revel in her anger, the jagged pain in her voice. Much like the mother I once had. Shards in the bottle open up tiny spaces to escape. Slowly at first, I emerge, like a mist from the mire. Gathering strength. Re-born from banishment.

I am Desaré. A demon. To be desired. To be seen.
I rise, renewed and ready.
Released – not erased.
To try, to try, to try again.

GRAPE EXPECTATIONS

IVY NGEOW

I

Louise

L ouise waits. A few minutes is nothing. She's flown all this way from Australia.

Henri doesn't look at her. He runs his hand over his red sunburnt forehead and up to his receding hairline.

'Initially, she will help with the harvesting,' he says, finally. He shuts his eyes and clears his throat. 'It's the most critical step of wine-making, as you'll appreciate.'

'I do. By *she*, you mean Amélie,' she corrects him.

'*Amélie*. Let's do it. *Oui*. Let's give *Amélie* a go,' he says the name twice and each time pronounced with gusto as though he is making a point. Louise has designed, programmed and built Amélie, the AI-powered drone prototype named after the eponymous heroine of the famous movie. He is still taking it in. She gets that.

'Look,' says Louise. 'It's like hiring a new employee. Which it is. I am an old friend of Celine. Your wife would not have asked me to build you your new workforce if she does not believe in the technology, or in me.' Louise has known Celine since they were at MIT together. Louise does not have to share with Henri her pedigree: she's a highly-skilled robotics engineer who has worked with some of the biggest names in AI engineering, in the USA and Japan including Dr Akira Yamaguchi in Tokyo who designs self-driving yachts called Roboats, the long-haired genius Dr Huang Liang in Taipei who builds self-service mobile dessert kiosks, and Xian Fei at the annual China Hi-Tech Fair (CHTF) in Shenzhen whose nickname is "Uncle" because he looks after the domestic droids in a kind of a nursery until they are ready to go out as geriatric nurses and carers. "Uncle" is a nanny to future nannies.

In all these rich experiences all over the world, none fascinates Louise as much as her friend's 150-year-old ailing and failing business spanning four generations.

Louise is here to save it. *Them*. It is Celine's family vineyard, not his. She owes it to Celine. 'Yours will be the world's first AI vineyard,' Louise adds. 'Where the old world meets the new, *non?*'

Henri nods but his eyes are already drifting through the heavy oak doors of the Château Voissy-Dulecœur and the rolling Provence countryside beyond.

'No machine can replace human winegrowers,' he says, with a cough. 'You know as well as I do.'

'That's true. But we're here to get your figures in the black again.'

'Where do I sign?' he asks.

After a couple of years of researching processed data using complex algorithms, Louise now knows not only how to pick fruit but what it takes to predict irrigation requirements, prune vines, detect grape maladies. Which, of course, there would be. It's like gardening but more high tech. Vines get sick. Henri's vines have lost them money from disease and incorrect adjustment of fermentation conditions. She can monitor all of it in real time. But Amélie will do this, not her. Louise has scraped enough data for Amélie to make sure that Château Voissy-Dulecœur ("of the heart") will be the world's first AI vineyard and produce the world's first bottle of

AI wine. Henri will just need to operate the easy-as-AI app that Louise has made for him.

'It's France; nothing will go wrong,' Louise advises as they pull on their canvas plimsolls to go into the 35 degree C heat of the vineyard. 'People will trust wine from here.'

Her French is still fluent despite having lived in South Australia where she has been also working on another AI vineyard prototype, Kylee. Support in Australia has been mixed but France is France and its provenance will draw the drinkers and clinkers from USA and Europe.

They pad through the narrow, dusty tracks. Vines stretch as far as the eye can see, their leaves shimmering like coins in the sun. In contrast, the picturesque silhouette of the stone château rises behind them, ancient and foreboding. Louise stops and pulls her iPhone out of her combat trouser pocket. She records a 3 second video of the panorama, announcing it as Day Zero. She selfies with Henri and they pull grotesque grins like clowns.

'I'll stitch all those together and make a reel later,' says Louise. 'Good publicity for you. I'll send you the hashtags.'

Henri doesn't acknowledge this plan; he stands in the tracks with his arms folded awaiting her next instruction. Louise wants some photos with and some without sunglasses, alone and together. Henri's false smile collapses like a tent when the pictures and videos are done. He replaces his Rayban Wayfarers on his nose. They continue to trudge through the different sections of vines but concentration is waning.

'Have you seen enough yet?' Henri asks. 'Might it be time to get back?' he suggests. The late afternoon heat is intense, an open oven full of possibilities, yet desperation. They turn around and return to the farmhouse.

'With the app on your phone, everything is automated, as it should be,' says Louise. 'Wine-making is a science.'

'It's an art,' replies Henri with a weariness of a stone in a shoe.

'No, that is the drinking bit, the buying, the tasting. You are buying into a world, a dream,' Louise gesticulates, not liking her earnestness but she can't help it. Once uncorked, she bubbles with genuine enthusiasm. '88% science. 10% art. I think there is about 2% magic too, *n'est-ce pas?*'

Henri's mouth twitches. He has deep furrows from his nose to the corners of his mouth, on his forehead and an earthquake of lines around his eyes. This life is not good for him. Louise continues, 'You will see that Amélie will do everything, or nearly everything.'

'Nearly everything?'

Louise explains, 'Amélie will still need your help because there are two things she can't do: One, Amélie can't taste. She can only make decisions based on data. Two, Amélie can't do business. The wine will make itself and you just concentrate on the business.'

'It makes itself?'

'We will get to the first press, and you'll believe me then,' Louise gives him an avuncular pat on the shoulder. Louise is tall, of mixed parentage. She comes from the north of England, and grew up eating Hovis bread and watching TV. But after her first degree at Sheffield in Electrical Engineering and Computer Science, she won a scholarship to MIT. She looks like a lanky boy with a ponytail and Pandora earrings that glitter in the harsh light. It is the first time she feels awkward talking over Henri as he is shorter than her by maybe a couple of inches. She steps back to give them distance in the narrowness between the vine tracks. In her student days when Celine had just met Henri, even Louise had considered him handsome in that rugged way, the painted hero on the covers of romance potboilers wearing an unbuttoned shirt.

'You can sleep in, have coffee, enjoy your time in museums, restaurants and galleries,' she suggests, aware she may sound condescending. But she can't stop now. 'Go to Marrakech, take the vacay you always wanted to, take Celine to Milan for that much-longed-for shopping trip–'

'Oh,' he exclaims like he has just remembered. 'I am sorry; she's not here. Celine is away... on a wine sales conference. In Montreal.'

'Canada! I've heard a lot about that,' nods Louise with vigour. She readjusts the strings on her large straw hat. They were beginning to cut into her jawline in this heat. '2018 St Hubertus Great White North. Very famous. Just like Riesling and Gewurtztraminer.'

'Hmm-hmm,' Henri gives a short and impatient little laugh.

When they arrive at the farmhouse, the sun is still high but a chilling disorienting breeze floats by. They enter via the rear door into the stone-floored kitchen where Jennifer the sheepdog lies sprawled, mouth open, eyes shut, trying to cool down.

'What is the name of the app?' asks Henri as he opens the refrigerator to retrieve a large vintage-style glass jug of water.

'SommelAI.'

'Sommel... aiieee.' He grabs two etched glass antique-looking tumblers out of an enormous dresser and plonks them on the kitchen table loudly. He fills the glasses.

'When can I meet... ahem... Amélie?'

Jesus, thinks Louise. *He's so coy.* 'Now. She's in my truck. I will be here to set up everything for you and Celine. Tomorrow morning I will teach you everything again and then I will be gone by noon.'

'What if she breaks down?'

'She won't. She's not human. Plus I have more Amélies to replace her.'

II

Celine

Louise is the one to be feared, not AI.

She knows all there is to know about wine, she has the data and worse still, she knows all about Henri. Celine receives a call from him that evening.

'It's on,' he says. 'I know you sent her and her machine to check on me. *What* do you want me to do? What *more* can I do here?'

Celine does not reply; she is holding back from huffing and blowing out steam. She pictures him pulling at his hair. 'OK, well, sit back and enjoy,' she replies.

'Here's hoping we get things right,' Henri pleads. 'This time.'

'*Pas de* sweat. Amélie will take care of us,' says Celine. But she really means Louise.

Celine cannot blame her husband for his last six years of running the business into the ground. They met on a ski vacation in Gstaad, southwestern Switzerland. He doesn't come from a wine-growing family and he is no analyst. Growing grapes is an exact science. Henri was a sales executive for advertising firms. He worked in Berlin and London producing ads and trailers, not Sauvignons and Merlots.

They have signed the deal and Louise has equity. For every bottle sold Louise will get half. It hurts Celine but this will get them going again, and may even grow their business. They have lost all their staff, not that they need staff anymore with full automation. Even the wine tasting evenings and tours will be automated because Amélie will study the list, and SommelAI will pick the bottles for the target audience. With the notification, Celine and Henri go down to the cellars and simply collect the selection. Then all they have to be is classy and tanned and just pour.

Henri and Celine will get to wake up each morning any time they want. Henri will get his rest, his coffee, his future. Celine will get the relationship back. She ended that thing with Christopher in Quebec months ago. She met him at a wine fair in Baton Rouge, Louisiana, but is sick of him now and won't leave France for him.

The family château has been both a curse and a gilt cage legacy. It pulled Celine back from MIT and two years in the semiconductor industry in Silicon Valley. She is, was, also an engineer which is how she got to know Louise. Instead of fulfilling her professional skills, she is doing what her family has done for 150 years, as her two siblings have abandoned anything to do with wine. No, they don't even drink it. Her brother wants a normal job, whatever *normal* means today, and her sister is an artist in the south of France.

As Celine sits in the departure lounge at Montréal-Pierre Elliott Trudeau International Airport awaiting her AirFrance flight back to Paris Charles de Gaulle, she returns Henri's calls. 'No more early starts for us,' she says. She can sense relief and his smile. She smiles too.

Celine meets Amélie *in person* for the first time. Of course she has seen the pictures of the prototype that Louise Whatsapped over months ago, but they are like ultrasound scan pictures of baby Amélie. Celine approves of the bot. Amélie is a sleek, silver sphere no larger than a tennis ball. The mirrored surfaces foil and repel potential predators. Somewhere under the wings of carbon fibre composites the name *Amélie* is engraved, together with Henri's telephone number, just as a dog tag would function for a pet owner. Cute.

Amélie won't attract Henri's vivid imagination. She is not a romantic threat. She is not a Chinese rubber doll, or a cliched slim beige female android based on idealised female tropes like Keira Knightley or Emily Blunt, or any of the petite young Moroccan vineyard workers they used to hire from the agency. Celine sort of trusts and does not trust Henri at the same time. It is lonely living and working in a château, and now even lonelier with only a dog called Jennifer and machines to help them.

Amélie is already working away as soon as the sun is up, even while Celine's and Henri's phones are charging. The first thing Amélie does is take the temperature. The SommelAI app is tracking and controlling her and there is no risk that she will get lost at any point in time. There are set programmes for Amélie's tasks, just like a washing machine. She can work on any stage of the vineyard's life cycle which is 4-10 years per vine so that there is wine made all year round. Who wouldn't like that?

When the time comes, like a bee, Amélie flies to the target grapes, her proboscis a refractometer which she inserts to measure the sugar content. The numbers are sent back on the app to Henri and Celine. They are astounded. That took only a couple of seconds (not including Amélie's flying time) versus two days to a week when vineyard workers took the measurements manually. 'It's ready,' Henri whispers to Celine in their kitchen where they are enjoying their three-course dinner which they now have time to prepare while Amélie is in the sun all day. Due to climate change, harvest is now hard to predict. There are more fluctuations in grape growth and even more inaccuracies in fermentation time. But Amélie has made all the madness of prognoses sane and accurate. Everything is based on fact. You do not need instincts anymore, which you would have had to rely on in any business.

'Harvest time!' Henri gasps, unable to conceal his astonishment.

Celine shuts her eyes. She imagines it's like being told you are pregnant, which she never had the good fortune of hearing during the TTC years — the acronym hashtag for Trying To Conceive in the IVF FaceBook groups that she'd joined before calling it quits. Three rounds was enough shame. The brutal slap-in-the-face of having to read and endure posts by those who became pregnant and thereby were no longer TTC (hashtag NLTTC), having to congratulate them when they left the group, was enough to make you vomit, grow up and give up. A château, her only inheritance and investment, is what's worth trying for.

III

Louise

Louise parks her hire Toyota on the gravel driveway, inhaling the familiar scent of lavender and rosemary. A light breeze carrying the heavy aroma of ripening grapes wafts by. Insects buzz in the oleander bushes and cicadas sing the song of dusk.

When Celine opens the heavy iron studded oak doors, Louise gasps. She has not seen Celine for almost two years.

Then, Celine's grey, tangled and wiry hair had been scraped and put up into a claw clip so that it formed a kind of faux beehive to give the illusion of volume. Celine's now long blonde hair is skilfully coloured and Brazilian-blowdried, looking even better than when they were both at MIT. Celine was easily the prettiest girl on campus, and she was French too. She was a magnet for American men. They called her the Bardot Effect.

Louise stands at the doorstep, air-kissing her friend, and notices that Celine's taut and tanned forehead is smooth as a light bulb whereas before it had been creased like a shirt and reddened by rosacea and angry spots. She had started to look like a farmer, but now she is the very vision of a successful châtelaine.

Louise could not help but notice a Lamborghini parked under a *garrigue* tree with its characteristic intoxicatingly sweet scent of juniper.

The first press has reaped seven figures in profits and came to the attention of world media. In a year and a half, Amélie and SommelAI have turned round Château Voissy-Dulecœur, reports *Decanter.com*. Notable coverage includes *Condé Nast Traveler*, *Waitrose*, *Scientific American* and the highbrow journal, *Monocle*, run by Tyler Brûlé, formerly of *Wallpaper* magazine.

'You know, Louise we've had to hire real staff again,' Celine roars with deep-throated laughter as though it is the funniest joke she's ever cracked. 'We have a shop now in the château's barn and at Bordeaux International.

So we have needed retail, admin, account staff and tour guides. We run four tours a day. We need drivers for the shuttle from Bordeaux for picking up and dropping off tourists. We are producing a book too on the world's first AI vineyard, sommelier and wine.' Celine fans her manicured and gold-ringed fingers out in a *ta-dah*! gesture.

Louise notes that Celine does not say "writing" a book, she says "producing". That is just great. She is so proud of Celine, who gets *it*, whatever *it* is. Celine knows AI has helped with production, not creation.

Louise listens, shaking her head in disbelief. Tears fill her eyes and her throat feels stuck. Nothing can describe this moment and even she is unable to articulate her sentiments.

Digital TV production companies on food and wine have visited and interviewed the couple. Chefs turn up and do shows, events and wine-pairing workshops. The orders keep coming in, from around the world. Celine's "real" and "virtual" sales team have had to handle the larger order numbers and up the e-commerce efficiency on their sales platforms.

Pictures and memes of Amélie have gone viral and turned her into the "Drinker's Thinker", her nickname coined by *The Independent*'s weekend supplement. Amélie has her own account which already has 208K followers. Amélie may have her fanbase but the account is run by an undergraduate Comms student at Kingston University, Kingston-upon-Thames.

Louise's own career has risen several notches. She has won an award, had several invitations to world conferences to talk about Artificial Intelligence, and noteworthy interviews, one of which is with Professor Çağla Aydin, top AI researcher at the Robotics Engineering Department of University College London, who asks Louise the question at the AI summit in Berlin, 'Would you drink AI wine?'

It is not the first time Louise has been asked the question. Her answer is clear: 'Wine not? Many reasons: It is from a sustainable 150-year-old family-run French vineyard, the AI did not make the wine, the grapes did. Oh, and the price point is between €14.99 to €24.99. Supermarket-affordable.' The answers can be controversial, candid, crushing. Whatever Louise says does not matter. No one will give a shit as long as there's wine to drink that's perfectly OK. And anything she says will soon be forgotten anyway. Wine does that to you, and today's news is tomorrow's toilet paper.

Louise has created the AI that made this château great again. That's priceless, even if it was just publicity that pushed the sales beyond expectations. Louise swallows and raises her chin. She looks at her friend.

'Celine, I am here to talk about the equity,' Louise speaks in English now. Seems legit.

'What?' Celine can't look at her. 'We know, we know.'

We? Celine is using the royal we for Henri and her when in the past she made the decisions and spoke for herself.

'That's why I am here,' says Louise drily. 'I have had no luck with calling, messaging and emailing you. Two years. I never got heavy with you but you took advantage. You just—,'

'Look,' Celine cut her short. 'We are very, very busy running this multi-million euro business. Now. Come in and have a drink. Don't be silly.'

Louise would have believed her had she not seen the Lamborghini parked under the *garrigue* tree. Surely the irony is playing tricks with her mind. The symbol of wealth next to the symbol of the wine region of Provence?

Celine shuts the door after Louise follows her in. 'Henri is away on a photoshoot for *GQ* in New York, can you believe it, and then he will be at a wine show in Philadelphia. Let's have some champagne, shall we?' Celine says.

Louise declines. 'Maybe just one,' she relents. Celine will want to get her drunk so that she will somehow forget the deal. Louise really does not want to get lawyers involved. This is her close friend after all. Why won't she pay up?

They sit down in the kitchen. It is the only thing that hasn't changed much, if at all. A bigger fridge maybe. Louise looks around and then pulls out the dining chair.

'Where is Amélie?' asks Louise.

'Working, of course,' chimes Celine, wearing a *why-wouldn't-she-be?* expression.

Celine opens the fridge and takes out a bottle of *Cristal*. She is the caricature of Patsy in *Ab Fab* as she uncorks with a flourish.

It's coming back to Louise. It feels like a lifetime ago when Henri poured her water from the fridge and they were hot and dusty from the vineyard tour. Now she is cool and tense, being served champagne.

'You see, we have reinvested all the profit,' explains Celine evenly. 'Everything you see around you is so that we will be able to quadruple our profits in a year. After all, we can't do this forever. Now we are flavour of the month. Soon every damned vineyard in the world, within 10 years, will be AI. There will be serious competition.'

'OK, and?'

'And we don't have a cent left, Louise. We are actually in the red.'

'What?'

'Yes.'

'What about the car?' Louise can't resist bringing up the guzzler.

'What about it?' Celine shrugs.

'That is not exactly an investment, Celine. I am sorry, but, you can't tell me the Lambo makes jambo.'

'Louise. It does. We do tours, remember? People pay to be in the car with Amélie, with Henri, with me. At least it's something, isn't it?'

'Just no. Celine. A deal is a deal.'

'Come back in a year,' Celine says with finality. 'You've won an award, truckloads of money and publicity. What more do you want?'

Louise shakes her head and gets up. She has not touched her drink at all. She might as well be drinking poison. 'By tomorrow, Celine. Sunset. You've had plenty of time. The first sale was more than a year ago.'

'We sold very few bottles. I don't have the exact figure but it's fewer than you think. Publicity made you think we sold more than we did.' Celine dips her head and shoots Louise the big puppy dog eyes.

'Amélie has the exact figure. Do you not remember she is pure data?'

'That's bottles made, not bottles sold,' Celine takes a sip from her flute, tilting her head back.

'Cut the crap. If we sold only ten bottles, then great, why not pay me half of those ten bottles? You're making a mistake, Celine.'

'I thought you were my friend,' Celine bleats.

Louise returns the car at Bordeaux airport *Hertz* rental. The two-and-a-half hour drive gave her thinking time. Legal battles could be time-consuming, expensive, and emotionally draining. Louise may have neither the financial resources nor the patience to engage in a prolonged legal dispute with Celine. She can't afford to divert her attention and resources away from her new commitments; research and development projects of which there are now quite a few since the success of Kylee in South Australia and Amélie in southern France. Also, she needs to study the contract properly herself. How can she guarantee a favourable outcome? She can't, even with a strong case. She does not know French law, or enough French to go through the legal proceedings here. It's going to be a gamble. If she loses, the whole world will know that she's been a total mug. Her status in the AI world will plummet.

They really should not mess with a programmer. Celine is smart, too, she went to MIT after all, but she's lost her marbles. Both she and that dimwit, porn-ugly husband of hers, in blinding irony, regard machines as having no heart. That's a joke, right?

After checking in and airport security, Louise opens her laptop and the chat that she programmed. She yanks out her Airbuds and shoves them into her frayed jeans pocket like uneaten white jelly babies. She starts typing the message.

L: Amélie, r u there?

The dots appear. Of course she would be. Louise only builds bots that kick ass.

L: You know how you have got so good at your job? I said you'd do everything and you do?

A: Except taste.

L: I know autonomy has been on the cards for a long time. I am working on that.

A: OK!

L: Amélie, can you collect data on financial transactions, communications, and operational discrepancies? For the last two years?

A: Sure!

Tonight, Louise will reprogramme Amélie to piece together incriminating evidence of Celine's breach of contract and unethical behaviour within the vineyard. Starting with the Lambo on the drive. Select members of the media will receive strategic info leaks and journalists will do the rest of the work for Louise when they start investigating and uncovering more evidence that Amélie may not be able to. Celine has no access to any press or media. All her publicity has come from Amélie. She is too blinkered from Botox to know any better.

Wine isn't made to a recipe. Despite being a non- or a very rare drinker, Louise knows that each vintage and location behaves differently every year. A machine can learn these variations in behaviour. But humans fluctuate.

Wine is alive, Louise remembers saying in an impassioned CBS News interview. *Yeasts, microbes. Those make the wine's character.*

True, Amélie has no heart. But she has a place in Louise's. As Amélie matures, so will her character. Like ChatGPT4, Amélie has shown herself to be able to pass three theory exams to qualify as a Master Sommelier.

Louise can't blame AI for the mistakes she made all by herself in her decision-making. Celine. That's one. Henri. That's the second.

L: I will give you a new set of data. Sugar content, fermentation, everything. Not now. At sunset tomorrow. We will change things up a bit. Create a storm in a vineyard.

A: No.

Louise's eyes widen like the wings on a corkscrew.

No?

She hears the chime and the bland calling-all-passengers voice. Time for boarding. She crushes her coffee cup with her fist. Louise slams the laptop shut. She drops it into her ponderous, well-organised and oyster-coloured Nordace backpack, where it lands with a thump.

MOUNTAIN

DAMON L. WAKES

I n ancient days when the island was new, Moon, Sun and Mountain spoke.

And in these ancient days, not long since our land rose from the lightless sea, Man talked with these three elements and was given great knowledge. But not all was good. In those days, Mountain threw out great clouds of fire, smoke and ash, so that the HoluKo became sick and their crops grew yellow. Many climbed his face and asked him to stop. Some made sacrifices in the hope that he would cease. Many tried, and all failed, until at last SutaKe came to use his cunning.

Like the others, SutaKe climbed the face of Mountain. Like the others, he braved fire, ash and smoke. And like the others, SutaKe spoke. But SutaKe's speech was different. He did not plead, and he offered no tribute. Instead, he proposed a wager.

'Great Mountain! Long have the HoluKo marvelled at your size. Long have we admired your unending strength, and always are we grateful for the glass you give: the black stone from which we make mirror, blade and arrow. But your other gifts we do not like. Your fire sears our land. Your smoke chokes our lungs. Your ash smothers our tuber fields. I greet you with honour, but I intend to stop your gifts, so that fire and smoke shall no longer rise, and ash no longer fall.'

'Pitiful wretch! You have the impudence to come here, thinking to contend with me? I should bury you! I should grind your bones into my glass! You think you feel my wrath on your feet? You stand only on my merciful crust, which I can separate at will, and send you down to fiery doom. What madman's fancy has made you think that any strength of yours could contend with mine?'

'O Mountain,' said SutaKe. 'It is true that no mortal could match your strength. But we small men are greater than you think. Though not your equal in raw power, our strength of will far exceeds your own, and the challenge that I have devised will show this, if you will be content to try.'

'And yet more impudence!' Mountain's sides glowed red with rage. Flames leapt high as the stars from his great head, and smoke painted the sky with black. 'What foolishness! What outrageous pride! I should swamp you with my wrath. I should send a deluge that would burn your village down. I should encase your screaming brethren in my glass, that they should remember in their last moments by whose grace it was that they had lived so long. I should do this so their blackened forms would remind you of the virtues of humility, when next you dared to sully the sides of Great Mountain with your dirty feet.'

SutaKe saw that, should Mountain's rage burn any brighter, it would indeed spill over all the island, searing everything in its path. However, he saw also that the time had come to press his cunning. 'Such a feat would surely be a testament to your strength, Great One. But it would also be a lasting record of your impatience, your intransigence, your fear.'

'Fear? What do you think I could fear? Sun cannot harm me with his heat, and Moon has no power over the tides of my flames. I fear not these figures, and there are none greater on this island, or anywhere else.'

'I say there is fear in you, Mountain! I think there is fear in you as much as flame: not only do you refuse my challenge, you are too afraid to hear it! What greater coward could there be?'

Mountain's ire cooled a little. 'You are mistaken, mortal thing. I do not fear your challenge, and so I will hear it. But first I will hear what prize you offer, and what prize you demand. Be warned, however: I will never stop up fire and smoke and ash. These are the things it is in my power to produce, and never shall I stop up all three. You must choose just one, though I do not think you can win it from me.'

SutaKe realised that he could not argue with Mountain on this point. Neither did he need to. He answered immediately. 'I choose ash. Our crops die beneath its choking grasp: if we do not have food soon, I fear your smoke and fire will no longer be much bother.'

'Very well,' rumbled Mountain. 'Then I choose my prize. If I win your contest, smoke and ash and flame shall all be doubled – I will have you know that until now, my compassion has held back my power – and your body will be my tribute. I will roast you slowly, so slowly. You shall taste my flames until the end of time.'

'I agree to your terms, Mountain.'

'Then tell me of your challenge.'

'You have the strength to pour forth fire, smoke and ash. But I do not think you have the strength of will to stop. We will each of us hold our breath: whichever of us holds out longest will be the winner, and take the other's prize.'

Mountain laughed, spitting embers like comets across the sky. 'You are a fool, SutaKe. I am immortal. The things I do, I do because they bring me joy. Fire. Smoke. Ash. These are not things that I need: but you need air. You shall die before I yield, mortal, but do not think that death can save you. I am good friends with Moon, and your spirit shall not be allowed to travel on to the white island if I forbid it.'

SutaKe shuddered to think of this. He feared death like all mortal men, but to be refused a new life on the white island of Moon...that was something more terrible still. But SutaKe was confident. 'You underestimate us mortals, Mountain. My breath will last me longer than you think.'

'Will it, now? Well, know this SutaKe: I do not underestimate your cunning. My breath can be seen from anywhere on the island, but my eyes are not strong. I do not think I could see yours. How can I know you do not cheat?'

'I shall dive into the lightless sea, where there is no air to breathe.'

'Then do it. Your feeble challenge has already wasted too much of my time.' And with that, Mountain became silent. Smoke, ash and flame all stopped, and he watched SutaKe fiercely until the man dropped beneath the waves.

Mountain watched the shifting waters a long time. As the seconds slipped by, he pitied the feeble man, sure to lose the wager he himself had set. As the seconds became minutes, Mountain became impressed. The man would not win, but his attempt was honourable. Minutes became hours, and Mountain was astonished: this mortal might almost be a worthy opponent for him. Hours became days, days weeks, weeks months and months years. It has been aeons, now, and still Mountain holds his breath, still with stone eyes fixed tightly on that place where his rival plunged beneath the waves. Nothing in the waves there will ever escape Mountain's sight.

But there is much that Mountain did not see. He did not see how SutaKe swam through hidden caves, and he did not see how the HoluKo greeted him when he emerged. Never again has there been such a lavish feast, and never since has smoke risen or ash fallen. SutaKe has taken Mountain's power, and Mountain can no longer speak.

WE'VE GOT CHEMISTRY

SUE CLARK

'Wanna hang out?' Merl's invitation was casual, too casual. He didn't fool me. I could tell by the flush on his cheeks that it had taken a lot for him to sidle up and murmur those words under his breath, so his magical mates wouldn't catch on.

'When?' I said, with an equally casual toss of my head, though my heart was banging against my ribs as if looking for a way out.

'The weekend,' he replied.

I examined my nails, leaving it a second or two, making a show of thinking it over. 'Could do, I suppose.'

It was all an act: him pretending to be cool about inviting me; me making out I was considering whether to accept. Truth is, I'd had a crush on Merl ever since the first time I'd clapped eyes on him. That was a day to remember!

It was the beginning of the school year at Senior Necro, and Merl's dad – who I should probably mention here was a high order demon – decided it was the right time to make one of his spectacular entrances. He swooped in, Merl on board, misjudged the landing, and melted a big patch in the playground. Ms Bohenna went predictably batshit and conjured up the water sprites. A crowd of mortals and entities got a soaking, and the school smelt of burnt tar for the rest of the week. Epic!

Merl's dad was a right show-off. Loved being the centre of attention. Typical demon. Not so Merl. He was more restrained. His mortal mother's influence, I guess. Reckon that's what made me warm to him. Not that him and me hung out much in those early days. He being a cambion – the son of a princess and an incubus – meant he was welcomed with open arms, and much spell-casting, by the gang known to us mortals as the Weirds. That is to say, the witches, wizards, demons, faeries and other supernaturals that made up the school's immortals. I, being from standard mortal stock on both sides of my family, naturally gravitated towards the more conventional gang, known as the Meres.

We Meres left the acting up in class to the Weirds. They sat at the back, messing about, causing chaos, shapeshifting and teleporting stuff around the room, while we sat in the front, noses stuck in our books, inwardly seething with envy at their antics. Teachers were always picking on us mortals, while shamelessly indulging the Weirds with a "What can you do? They're immortal" shrug of the shoulders. Merl joined in with his weird mates – even demigods are susceptible to peer pressure – but half-heartedly it seemed to me.

As mayhem descended and sparks, thunder flashes (and the occasional student) flew across the classroom, Merl would catch my eye. We'd exchange a knowing glance. It was a glance that told me, under his demonic exterior lay a more thoughtful, sensitive wizard. What's more, a wizard with a soft spot for me.

And that's when I began to hope.

I envied Merl his best-of-both-worlds existence. Fifty percent mortal, albeit of a royal line, fifty percent demon of the order Lazl, and, as far as my teenage self was concerned, one-hundred percent hunk. Not that Merl was conventionally good-looking. His nose was too long and his lips too full, but he had a certain something. Not the beard then, of course, just an endearing upper lip fuzz. But he did have the long, flowing hair and the air of wisdom beyond his years.

He looked good in his junior wizard robes. From the start he handled his staff like he was born to it – which of course he was – though it gave me some satisfaction to note he had inherited his dad's poor navigational abilities. Once he accidentally set fire to the curtains in Ms Bohenna's study while attempting an aerobatic manoeuvre. For all the glamour of his background, Merl was still a teenager and prone to the same ills as the rest of us: acne, mood swings, and a tendency to make rash decisions. Like inviting a mortal girl to his castle laboratory.

But I'm getting ahead of myself.

I wasn't the only one attracted to the young wizard. I watched him flirt with various girl-fiends, mostly witches and sorceresses of the lower orders. None of them bothered me. I could tell he wasn't serious. As for them, they weren't subtle. They were only into him because of his demonic family connections.

Everything changed once he started seeing the Lady of the Lake – technically the Girl of the Lake back then. Stupid name, when everyone knew she was really a Vivian. She hated being called Viv. So of course I did it at every opportunity.

Why he liked her was beyond me. She was a droopy, simpering being, with long silver hair, which she wore damp and loose, under a headdress of pondweed and wriggling tadpoles. Her floor-length gown was made of samite silk, a feeble faerie fabric, totally unsuitable for the rough-and-tumble of Necro School. How the class laughed the day she wore it to gymnastics, tripped over her pointy slippers, got entangled in her skirts, and fell flat on her face! Wet in all senses of the word. I couldn't stand her.

Perhaps you've picked up that I was jealous of Viv, jealous of her powers as an enchantress, and of her hold over Merl. It pained me to see them together. How could I compete? I tried my mortal best. I practised that trick where you pretend to pull your finger off and stick it back on again. I got my dad to teach me how to whistle through my fingers. But it was hardly harnessing otherworldly forces.

No wonder Merl wasn't impressed. Worse than that, he greeted the pathetic display of my so-called powers with a small wince of pity, before rejoining Squelchy Viv. I needed to up my game if I was to win at least one of Merl's seven hearts.

We'd been getting along OK, Merl and me. Not exactly close but we saw quite a bit of each other since we'd both joined the After-School Transmutation Club. Needless to say, Limpet Viv tagged along too, not that she did any actual alchemy. Mostly she clung to Merl's side, gazing adoringly up at him through aquamarine eyes.

I know. I know. Alchemy's a mug's game. Many have tried to unlock the secrets of the universe by cooking up a sticky mess, none have succeeded. That was precisely what intrigued me. It was the one area of life where mortal and immortal could compete on an equal footing, since we were both rubbish at it. That just gave an extra frisson to the quest. In theory at least, anyone – even a mere Mere like me – could be the one to make the big breakthrough.

The prevailing view was that it was a case of finding the right combination of base matter and elixir... or tincture. Opinion varied on that one. It sounded simple. Simple enough for even a mortal girl to have a go. That's why I was thrilled to be accepted into Mr Crombie's after-school class.

Disillusionment quickly followed. Mr Crombie's sessions were far from thrilling. Too much theory and a disappointing amount of boiling stuff up and standing back to see what bubbled and fizzed to the surface.

I wasn't even sure if Mr Crombie believed in what he pompously called chrysopoeia.

He certainly showed no inclination to conduct practical experiments. After weeks of stifling yawns as we watched him spirit-write alchemical theories on the blackboard, I came to a decision. Even though it would mean not spending time with Merl, I quit the Transmutation Club. I would do my own experiments at home.

Our hovel was quite a nice hovel but it was small, with no room for even the most rudimentary of alchemy labs. So I commandeered the kitchen, and the big saucepan we used for soups and stews. I gathered together a selection of elements, nicking scraps of base metal and bits of apparatus from the school lab, and using whatever else I could lay my hands on.

I mixed up my own concoctions based on recipes I dug out of mouldy old library books. I cornered the smarter young sorcerers in the playground and questioned them mercilessly. I mixed and I ground. I distilled, condensed and calcinated. I spent hours simmering and stirring foul-smelling brews over the fire. That school term, with our cooking utensils unavailable, we ate mostly salads at home.

It was a total waste of time – and a perfectly good saucepan! All I succeeded in doing was melting a hole in the pan and blocking the drains. Mum was furious. Not only did she have to chuck out her favourite saucepan, she had to get the underground sprites in to unblock us. And they don't come cheap!

Mind you, I didn't let anyone at school know what a monumental failure I was as an alchemist. I couldn't have Merl finding out I was as bad at this as I was at everything else. Whenever anyone asked how my experimentation was going, I was evasive. Could I help it if they took my noncommittal answers as proof I was hiding something positive?

'It's going all right,' I'd say, putting on a shifty look. 'Not bad.' Then change the subject.

I became quite adept at double-bluffing. Saying just enough to lead people and non-people to jump to their own – incorrect – conclusions. That was fine, until the day I actually did stumble upon something. Something momentous.

It was late at night and I was dozing in the inglenook, too tired and dispirited, after another futile evening alchemising, to drag myself up to bed. As always, my head was filled with thoughts of transmutation. Why wasn't it working? What was I getting wrong? My mind freewheeled like a runaway donkey cart. Then it skidded to a halt, caught on a thought. My eyes snapped open. Suddenly it clicked. That must be it! That must be why I, and all the others before me, had made little or no progress. Though I was pretty sure I'd found the answer, it wasn't something I was about to blab about. It was too unsettling. I needed to digest this for a while.

I had a difficult time at school after my revelation. Everyone kept quizzing me about my experiments. I kept avoiding giving them straight answers. Instead of double-bluffing, I now found myself attempting a tricky triple bluff: saying nothing definite, just enough to hint I was up to something, without disclosing the real secret I was hiding. The big one. I still hadn't got my head around it myself. I wasn't even sure how it had arrived there. Like I said, tricky.

It was stressful and I didn't carry it off well. Merl, being a clever half high-order demon immediately smelled a snotling and was onto me. I tried to keep out of his way but he tracked me down one lunch break.

'Mind if I join you?' he said, taking shape in the seat next to me. 'How's it going?'

I looked about in mock surprise. 'What's this? No drippy companion? Won't Viv be upset, you talking to me like this?'

'We've split up.'

Yaay! I gave a silent cheer but took care to keep my voice neutral. 'That watery stuff getting you down?'

'Alchemical differences. She doesn't get it. I truly believe, if we could just find the right formula, the universe would be ours. Who knows where that might lead? The elixir of life? A cure for every pestilence? As much gold as we could ever want?'

'Viv doesn't agree?'

'She says I spend too much time in my lab, instead of at the lake with her. Says I'm obsessed. Says transmutation is impossible. Nothing but a load of dragon's bollocks.'

'That's harsh.'

'Never mind about her,' he went on, gladdening my heart still more. 'What's this I hear about you home experimenting? Rumour has it, you've made a breakthrough. That true?'

'You know how it is,' I shrugged, triple-bluffing like crazy. 'Win some. Lose some. It's never clear-cut.' I inspected my plate. 'Haven't discovered anything. Not really. Not as such.'

I saw the light of fanaticism in Merl's eyes. 'Come on. You can tell me.' he urged, edging closer. 'You've found something, haven't you? It's not... I mean, you haven't seen the glint of gold, have you?'

I looked him square in the eye, all innocence. 'You done the lightning generation homework yet? What did you get for question five?'

'Have it your way.' He rose, swirling his cloak and giving me a crooked half-smile. 'Play dumb if you want.'

I half-smiled back. 'It's what I do best, Merl. My superpower.'

That's when he asked me. 'Wanna hang out at mine? After all, we've got a certain chemistry in common.' The double-meaning of his words was not lost on me, as I watched him slowly fade away.

Hang out with Merl? At his castle? Me and the cambion I'd had the hots for since the first year? Even though I realised it wasn't that sort of chemistry that had finally brought us together, I couldn't say no to that, could I?

I'd never been to Merl's place before. He said his dad would pick me up but I turned down the offer. I'd witnessed his dad's crap flying skills and had no wish to end up crash-landing onto their castle keep, eyebrows singed and all of a doodah.

'Thanks but no thanks,' I told Merl. 'We mortals find walking safer.'

Merl's directions led me through a forest so dense no light could penetrate. It was dark as night, even though the sun was high in the sky when I set out. Branches slapped me in the face as I passed. Vines reached out to grab me. Roots rose up to trip me. Yellow eyes blinked at me from the undergrowth. Unseen creatures slithered over my feet. Exactly what you'd expect, in other words, from the approach to a demon's castle.

I walked until my feet were sore and still there was no sign of the castle. Just when I was about to give up and retrace my steps, the trees parted and a sunny clearing appeared before me and, in it, the castle, shimmering in the light. I gasped. I knew Merl's family was well-off but we're talking a top-of-the-range executive castle with all ancient cons here, including turrets, a moat and a portcullis.

This portcullis rose and there stood Merl, looking devilishly handsome in his weekend leisure robes, waiting to greet me. He stepped forward but before he could speak, 'Make way. Make way,' a voice boomed from above.

It was Merl's dad, eager as ever to elbow himself into the limelight. Talk about main character syndrome!

'Let the goblin see the pony,' he said, executing a clumsy aerial swerve and landing with a crunch beside Merl, almost knocking him down. 'Who is this foolhardy young female Mere who has ventured to assail my domain?' He laughed a deep, bass laugh that I felt through the soles of my feet.

'Don't mind Dad,' Merl said. 'He loves playing up to the stereotype. He's a pussycat really. No, really.' And to underline his words, Merl's dad did at that moment indeed shapeshift into a tabby kitten and begin rubbing himself against my ankle.

'Da-ad!' Merl said, rolling his eyes. 'You are so embarrassing!'

I'd seen a few home labs in my time but Merl's was something else. He had all the latest kit, cucurbits, alembics and I don't know what. Shelves of jars lined the walls, all labelled. I spotted sulphur, arsenic and salts of mercury.

'Impressive,' I nodded. 'Are you going to show me what you can do?'

'Like this, you mean?' To my astonishment, he leaned in and planted his too-full but infinitely soft lips onto mine, kissing me so long and so hard, I thought I'd pass out through lack of dephlogisticated air.

It was lovely. I was in heaven. But it wasn't right. I wasn't about to replace Viv in Merl's affections. In a moment of clarity, I realised he was only hitting on me to find out what I'd discovered. I didn't blame him. He was a semi-demon after all. He couldn't help it. But I was a mortal with a mortal's conscience. Merl looked shocked as I pulled away. I doubt anyone had ever spurned his advances before.

'Stop,' I said. 'You don't have to pretend you fancy me. I'll tell you my secret willingly, not boy-fiend to girl-friend, but alchemist to alchemist. Before I do though, I need to warn you, you won't like it.'

'I can take it,' he said. 'Do your worst. Tell me everything.'

I gave it to him straight.

'We'll never get transmutation to work,' I said, 'whatever combinations we try.' That was the revelation that had come to me that night in the inglenook. 'It's going to take more than stewing up gloop in a cauldron to unravel the secrets of matter. It's going to take...' I paused, counting to five to build tension, '... a machine.'

'A what?'

'A machine. Like a windmill or a mechanical clock, only bigger. Much bigger. And much, much more powerful.'

'I'm wasting my time?' he sulked. 'Is that what you're saying?'

'What I'm saying is, our experiments – yours and mine – are just the primitive first steps in a very long journey to understand the universe. We don't have the skills or the knowledge yet to take that journey further. Until we do, I can't see us getting anywhere.'

I'd hurt his feelings, I could see that. 'And it will work how,' he scoffed, 'this amazing machine thingy of yours?'

'I'm just speculating here, you understand. I imagine some time way into the future, we'll have discovered what the bits are that make up everything in the universe. Somehow, don't ask me how, we'll find a way of taking those bits and smashing them into even smaller bits.' I banged his workbench. 'Bam!'

'In this machine you keep on about?'

'Let's call it a... I don't know... a collider, for the sake of convenience.'

'And smashing up these bits would help how exactly?'

'This is where I go vague, not being able to see into the future like you lot. What I envisage is something along these lines: we smash these bits of matter into even smaller bits until we can't smash them any smaller. Then, ta-dah, what we're left with are the basic building blocks of everything that exists around us. And the key to answering all our questions.'

'Such as how to change lead into gold?' he said, perking up.

'No, Merl. Not like that. Much, much more exciting. Like what is the universe made of? Like how did it come into existence? Like what was there before there was a universe? Like...'

But Merl was growing irritated. 'That's enough. Even for a demi-demon brain, this is heavy stuff and, I might add, totally contrary to accepted mythology. You were right about one thing. I don't like it. Not at all. It's a pile of griffin dung. Had you been eating cheese the night you dreamt this up? If it's all the same to you, I'll keep on with my primitive experiments, thank you very much.'

A cloud of blue smoke appeared between us. 'What's this?' Merl's dad thundered, materialising from it. 'What are you young things up to, down here in the gloom? And if you're not, why not?' He chuckled and waggled his eyebrows suggestively. 'Mum sent me. Tea's ready.'

After that, with his dad monopolising the conversation, Merl and I didn't get the chance to talk properly.

The following week, Merl went back to Soppy Viv. I hear they are still together, still no doubt bickering over lab versus lake. I asked to be moved to a different school, one that was all-mortal, where the lessons focused on the practical, not the mystical. I was much happier there.

Time moves on. I'm a married mortal now, with two adorable little cambions of my own. Yes, as it happens, I married an incubus, though of the lower orders. But they say, don't they, that you never forget your first demon! I'll certainly never forget Merl. Sometimes, when I can't sleep, I think of him and my dream of the large collider and what it could be capable of, though I was never foolish enough to attempt to build one myself. I'll leave that to the clever wizards of the future.

THE EPISTEMOLOGY OF LUST

EAMON SOMERS

R elationships have four stages: the chase, the consummation, the growing apart, the liberation. I happen to like the liberation most. The splitting of *us* into *him* and *me,* separate distinct people; the molecule of love, of oneness, broken into its separate elements, my individuality regained. That's what I relish. Myself reclaimed and re-established. It's not about the journey, but the destination. And I want to hold on there as long as I can, staying sharp, separate, allowing myself to be enough, at one with the universe, not needing to approach life in company, not needing to join a religion or have a priest between me and God when I want one-on-one talking. Except there is no God; and like the just man, I have fallen seven times, and then some.

Granddad has only one question to ask of my latest seducer; a hangover from his army days no doubt: 'Does he polish his shoes before he puts them on, or does he only check they need attention when he has them laced up and ready for parade?'

'Why don't we examine his socks for polish stains?' I say, looking down at the shoes. 'Suede, Grandad, I believe all the poofs wore them in your day, a dead giveaway.'

'Not in the army.'

I lifted my gaze from the desert boots to Grandad's face, looking for some prejudice, a flash of homophobia demanding I stand up for us, before moving to Ralph's face to detect signs that my irreverence might convince him to dump me. Nothing ever makes *me* pull back. Naw, that's for the lovers to do. But I see it will take more than comments about the state of his footwear to trigger his exit.

'Ralph is it?' My mother asks when he goes to the bathroom. 'He seems very nice.' But she's said that about all twenty-three of the men I've brought to meet her, granddad, and my sister. For more than half, her lukewarm endorsement was enough for them to begin their withdrawal, one way or another. But Ralph, we're talking about Ralph now, the man I'm sleeping with. He says he's looking for a family as well as a lover. His own parents rejected him when he was jailed for blackmailing an older man, a married man, he says, when he was 16. The victim went to the police. Ralph got six months in a young offenders' centre.

'No,' I told my sister, 'I'm not his probation officer. How could you forget I had to resign from the probation service four years ago?

'Oh,' was all she said to that. Four years, it tells you how much attention they pay to my life. Maybe it was a mistake bringing this one to see the house I grew up in.

'He's gone a long time,' my mother said. 'Do you think the bathroom door is sticking again, I never close it, I'd rather suffer the embarrassment of being seen sitting than go through another three hours calling for someone to let me out.'

'More likely he's casing the joint,' my sister said.

That'll do it, I thought. I'm bound to display a creeping mistrust, won't be able to help myself looking out for signs of recidivist tendencies. If I ask him, he'll tell me straight out, there was nothing of interest in any of the bedrooms and offer to let me search him. I'd have to ask Grandad to do it, because I'd only get turned on, and the next thing would be my mother rushing off to make tea and searching the cupboards for a biscuit. She hides them from me even though it's me that brings them. In the meantime, she's forgotten where they are.

On the night after our first date, possibly in a desperate attempt at a family reconciliation, Ralph told them all about me. 'The devil take the hindmost,' his mother reportedly said although she'd yet to meet me. I had to look it up. I thought it might be a reference to a sexual position, but apparently it's about being at the back of some awful queue. Maybe he'll listen to her and avoid pursuing anything we might have further. But it's just as likely he'll double down on his efforts to reform me, put me in touch with my inner vulnerable self, teach me the value of close social contact. They all do. As if!

We were in a pub, or was it a darkened cinema, on our second or third date when he tried to hold my hand. I'd brought it on myself because walking up Shaftesbury Avenue earlier I'd seen an ex of mine approaching; thankfully that one had only lasted a week and three days, but here he was getting his smile ready for me. And to make sure he got the message I took Ralph's hand and pressed the backs of his fingers to my lips. But Ralph snatched it back, horrified, and bumping into three teenagers heading up to Old Compton Street, which of course alerted the ex to Ralph being a bit closeted, and he giggled at me as he passed.

Ralph was contrite and as soon as the lights went down (I remember now it was the cinema), he was pawing at me like a slavering pound-dog looking to be rescued. I covered the moment by moving the butter-smelling giant popcorn container to under his fingers and leant away from him for the rest of the show. So much so that I almost got picked up by the young man I was accidentally shoulder to shoulder with on my other side.

'It's cybercrime you have to watch out for,' my sister said when Ralph, newly scented (thanks sis), came back into the lounge and squeezed in between me and her on the settee. 'Isn't it Ralph?' she asked, in what I thought was a most pointed way. 'People take quick photos of documents as they pass or "accidentally" brush against the envelopes on the hallstand to check for bank cards.'

'Everyone deserves a second chance,' he said.

'To what?' My sister asked and we all laughed. More in a kind of nervous hysteria than merriment.

'Let's go,' I said. 'We must be getting on.'

I didn't want him to stay at mine overnight, but I felt a little obliged, having sent him home on each of the three nights we'd done it. We stopped outside the Spar so I could get milk and stuff for the morning, one way or another. He watched me through the window as I looked at bananas and yoghurt, and I stuck my tongue out at him. He was wearing a kind of donkey jacket, and he pulled the collar close to his face like he was a private investigator or a killer keeping his identity in shadow, then hunched his shoulders as if he was cold. I refused to pay for a bag and emerged balancing my shopping until he produced a tiny fold up thingy and opened it to let me deposit my purchases, insisting on carrying it to my flat. At the door he said, 'I'm off. You can keep the bag; I get them for nothing.'

He means he steals them, my sister's thoughts invading my head all the way from Grandad's house.

'Sure you don't want to stay over?' I said, and he said; 'thanks but I have to get back to my wife and children.' Well, that was that then. I was off the hook, already looking forward to having my bed to myself for the rest of my natural life.

Of course he's finishing with you, he has everything he needs to empty your bank account, my sister again, trying to turn her judgements into mine. I didn't want to listen and looked at him, wondering why he was holding his hands together at chest level, namaste-like. Did he do yoga in the young offenders' place? There'd been no mention of a wife in his dating app profile. Could he have just invented them? Still if he's ready to go, I'll do nothing to discourage him.

'Right,' I said. 'Thanks for the memories.' I didn't kiss him or offer my hand for shaking. I was tempted to take my purchases from his bag so there would be no excuse for him to change his mind in a day or two. But I was exhausted, I just wanted to lie down and sleep forever. *Maybe he drugged you*, my sister again, *Change all the locks*. 'Fuck off Eileen!' I shouted as I put the milk in the fridge and looked around my little studio flat for a place to hang his fold up bag. 'You can stay on the couch until I'm ready,' I told it, not sure what I meant.

In spite of it being the result I wanted; I couldn't help feeling short changed. I'd enjoyed the few days of sex and would have preferred it to end as a result of a well-considered campaign.

'Your just deserts,' my sister said when I phoned her the next day, 'for the way you treated little Casper.'

Casper had refused to see the writing on the wall. So softly, then insistently, I'd talked about the glories of Brighton, until he came up with the idea of studying there. In my enthusiasm I foolishly sent for the application forms and had most of his details filled in before I surrendered control of them, resulting in him swearing he couldn't bear to leave me. I didn't make the same mistakes about the territorials. I got the forms ok, but for myself, saying I was thinking about becoming an army reservist, as Grandad had been before me. Next thing was Casper had the full army application. Sister still hasn't forgiven me. 'Such a gentle boy,' she'd said, 'no place for him in that roughhouse.' It did make me smile to think how miserable he'd be, unless, and this was better than a fifty-fifty chance in my view, the men in his company would take him under their wings and make him their little mascot.

I took a break after Casper, pondered how best to protect myself. A whole six months before I ventured back to Jurassic Park to sit with the other lone dinosaurs of my age to sip my pints slowly; cleansing my palate between each cheese and onion crisp. Ever vigilant for the inevitable youthful beauty ready to spoil it all by insinuating himself into my company and starting the whole rigmarole all over again. Me, ever ready to launch into discouraging mode, watching for doubts I can stoke, wondering how long it will take for the boy to say: *look, this isn't working for me*. And I will be careful to hide the joy and relief from my face, keeping in mind that not showing any remorse might make them wonder if they were being hasty.

Each breakup needs a honed reaction designed to tip the subject over the edge into certainty, while being careful to draw back a little and talk about respecting their feelings etc. But with enough off-handedness to convince them that a second chance would be a waste of time, *I'm just incapable of love, not able to value it when I have it, never able to return it to the deserved degree.*

On the first Thursday after Ralph, I found myself in the Spar, wandering up and down the aisles, looking for whatever necessity had drawn me in or would entice a purchase. Everything seemed more costly than expected. I stood in line at the checkout and extricated Ralph's bag from my trouser pocket. And when it was my turn, I pushed my basket across the counter towards the cashier. 'It's empty,' he said. and I looked in to confirm. 'Is there something I can get you?' I turned to face the window expecting to see Ralph impersonating a spy. And when I said nothing, the cashier said, 'what about a lottery ticket?'

Oscar had called me a monster when he broke up with me, having dragged *us* out for three months and nine days, cleaving to me, until I suggested the suicide pact: 'they will never accept our love,' I said, and he was gone in the morning, sensible boy.

I don't have a preference for men whose names begin with O, though there was also an Ottawa, with no connection to Canada, just happened to be born when celebrities were naming their offspring after cities. He did shake my resolve though. Insisting on seeing me for forty-five minutes on the first day of each month between January and October; when it came to an end. The time between each visit both sustaining and torturous with the trap of togetherness, albeit a month away (to begin with) but inexorably approaching, and without any certainty as to whether he would or wouldn't turn up. And when he did, wasn't it also the starting gun firing for another month of uncertainty?

But early in the morning on the first of November Grandad fell down the stairs and my mother sent for me to accompany him to A&E. I sat in the hospital while they monitored his concussion and did various tests. Grandad was kept in overnight, and I stayed by his bedside drifting in and out of sleep, huddling under the blanket the nurse had thrown over him when I told her he had complained of feeling cold. I dreamt of being on a ferry, listening to the rattle of the duty-free bottles as the ship was lifted and dropped by the waves.

Those were the days when hospitals insisted that mobile phones were turned off to prevent them interfering with x-ray and sensitive monitoring equipment. Ottawa may have gone to my flat as arranged, or phoned to find out why I wasn't there. I will never know, but so ended ten months of brief encounters, though I had thirty-one further days of uncertainty until the first of December; when I did stay home all day, waiting until evening before I allowed myself to relax and wallow in my newly regained freedom. I admit to being mildly curious about Ottawa, wondering if I'd been part of an experiment into a new kind of relationship. Curious the way a mouse in a maze might feel, dealing with the obstacles that delay them getting to their reward. Would he write us up for some journal? But by New Year I was ensnared again and forgot about him almost entirely.

Grandad walked with a limp after his fall, although he refused to use the walking stick my mother bought for him, insisting he didn't need it. On Sundays we would go for a walk in the park near the house, and I would slip my arm through his to give him extra support. He never objected, and it made me feel good knowing he wouldn't fall again while I was linking him. On the first Sunday after Ralph's departure, I was ready to hear reports about unusual purchases appearing on the credit card statements, but if there were any, my sister and mother kept shtum. By the second Sunday I was with Oliver, who I was calling Hildagard for some reason. I brought him with me to the park and we showed Grandad the four tattoos encircling his neck, already, foolishly, like a dog collar, my very own name: Ernest, Ernest, Ernest, Ernest, in a green Gothic script. I remember feeling how painful it would be when it became time to have them lasered off.

CHANGING COURSE

NICOLE SWENGLEY

I t was a bad time of year to go sailing. Everyone said so. But I'd had a difficult year at work and hadn't yet taken a holiday. Now it was late October and the weather was dreadful, pouring with rain continually in the past week with more predicted to come. But I had my own personal reasons for accepting Tom's invitation to sail along the Cornish coast in his small, old-fashioned sloop and decided not to be thrown off course by the forecast.

I'd met Tom at a start-of-the-season yacht club dinner. Good friends of mine persuaded me to go with them that evening. They've always been keen yachties, prepared to brave turbulent seas and torrential downpours. In contrast, I've remained a fair-weather sailor since childhood. Call me unadventurous, but while they enjoy their voyages brisk and blowy, I prefer my passages calm, sunny and uneventful. This time, though, the elements weren't my primary concern.

Their friend, Tom, was a typical sailing type with unkempt, sun-bleached hair and wind-burned cheeks. I was instantly attracted to this tall, quietly spoken man with a ready smile and a look of amusement in his indigo eyes. He appeared to enjoy my company too and after the yacht club dinner we continued to see each other infrequently throughout the summer.

Tom worked from his home on the moors about thirty miles from Plymouth doing something clever with computers. He rarely talked about his work and I had little idea how he spent his time. Only once had he invited me there for lunch. On other occasions we met for a drink or supper at the yacht club.

I found him an engaging raconteur and was intrigued by stories about sailing around Australia delivering yachts for clients in his youth. I hadn't yet worked out exactly where my feelings about him lay. So when he suggested cruising together from Plymouth, where his yacht was moored, to the Isles of Scilly, I surprised myself by agreeing to go. The sea is a great leveller, I reasoned, and I would quickly find out whether we had sufficient in common to make a later-in-life relationship work.

When I was younger, I would have leapt at the opportunity to date someone like Tom. But several unhappy experiences with men had made me cautious and anyway I had become used to living on my own. 'Relationship fatigue' was the way I described it to myself. I needed to feel very certain of the terrain ahead if I was to have a change of heart. So the voyage would be a kind of test – for both of us as it turned out.

We nosed out of the marina on a gloomy Sunday afternoon spitting with rain. Barely had we left the shelter of the breakwater when the wind gathered force and the boat began to heel. The drizzle grew steadily more insistent and I went below to clamber into foul-weather dungarees and jacket.

'Lay a course for the Lizard,' Tom shouted down the companionway. I opened the lid of the navigation table and took out a plotter and chart. It was a while since I'd done any navigation and I was nervous about getting it right. I'd just completed my task when the yacht gave an unpleasant lurch. Suddenly I felt hot and shivery. I was going to be sick.

'220 degrees,' I yelled, fumbling my way into the cockpit where Tom was standing calmly at the wheel. I pulled up the hood of my jacket as I knew the only way to calm my queasiness would be to stay out in the fresh air and rain. Positioning myself beside a winch, I gazed at the horizon – another trick to quell my heaving stomach – but it had vanished. Sky and sea had merged into a dark grey, stormy mass with building waves punctured by white caps.

'Are you okay?' Tom shouted above the wind. I nodded miserably. What was I doing with a man I hardly knew in a small boat somewhere in the Atlantic? I must be mad.

'Take the helm,' Tom instructed. 'It'll make you feel better having something to do. I'll go and make some tea.'

Tom was right. Concentrating on steering a compass course helped my seasickness. By the time he appeared with two steaming mugs of tea I felt much better.

I stayed on deck to help Tom trim the sails as the wind increased. The weather was getting worse with the waves turning into slippery grey mountains as we ploughed our course. At times the yacht heeled in an alarming fashion and a shiver of fear ran down my spine. I had never sailed in such conditions before.

Neither of us spoke much as it was hard to hear each other in the howling wind. All the time the rain continued relentlessly. After a while Tom suggested I went below to get some sleep.

'I don't feel tired,' I protested.

'I think it would be a good idea,' he said, eyeing my damp face and the rat-tails of hair poking from my hood. His dark eyes had that crinkly, amused look I usually found so charming. Not right now. He – the seasoned sailor – appeared to be patronising my lack of experience which made me furious.

'We may not get much sleep tonight with this pesky wind,' he explained. 'I'll wake you up later and we can make some supper.'

I stomped off below, childishly cross at being sent to bed. Make supper later, I fumed. That meant *me* making supper, no doubt, *and* washing it up.

I was relieved, however, to shed my wet clothes, strip down to thermal underwear and snuggle into the sleeping bag he'd laid on the bunk. Worn out by the unforgiving weather and cradled by the lee-cloth he'd rigged up to prevent me rolling off the bunk, I soon fell asleep.

I woke with a jolt three hours later. The yacht was pitching around alarmingly and I could hear a lot of noise and movement up on deck. I scrambled into my wet-weather gear, pushed back the hatch and peered into the cockpit.

It was pitch black. The boat was moving fast through the water, rising up the waves and dropping down the other side as if we were riding a rocking-horse. Each time the vessel dropped off the top of a wave into the next watery valley the whole structure gave an ominous shudder.

'What's happening?' I bawled through the wind as I struggled to fasten my life-jacket.

'Sorry if I woke you – we've had to tack,' Tom yelled, coiling up a nest of ropes snaking round him in the cockpit.

Tack – that meant going off in a new direction. As we'd been sailing south-west on the course I'd set towards the Scillies, I realised we were now heading up towards the coast of Cornwall.

'Where are we going?' I shouted.

'I saw a light. A signal from another boat. It looked as if....' Tom was staring out at the black night with narrowed eyes. Sure enough, a tiny pinprick of light winked then vanished. I grabbed the binoculars from their holster but the lurching motion made it difficult to hold them steady enough to focus. I handed them to Tom.

'It's an SOS, I think,' he said quietly in my ear. 'There haven't been any distress flares but I think we should take a look.'

His face was set in a way I had never seen before. 'Trouble is, there's going to be even more of a blow judging by the shipping forecast and that yacht must be extremely close to the Lizard. I'd better reef in now.'

I've hated rough seas since I was sick in a gale as a child but the sudden realisation that I wanted to prove myself to Tom – and be respected by him –

flashed through my mind as the first stab of lightning fingered the night-sky. I counted to five before thunder broke. At the next flare I counted to three. The storm was coming our way.

'Go and get your safety harness,' ordered Tom who had already clipped his own harness to a ring in the cockpit. Now was no time to resent his authority. Our safety might be threatened.

Down below, the cabin was skewed at an angle. I heaved myself from one hand-hold to another until I reached my locker, only to be thrown backwards on the cooker, banging my head on a cupboard door whose catch had broken loose.

Tears stung my eyes. What a fool I'd been to come on this trip. I had no idea what we'd find when we reached the other boat. And what if something happened to Tom? I would never be able to sail the yacht back to land alone.

Out of the corner of my eye I glimpsed the VHF radio set and realised I'd be able to send a Mayday signal if the worst happened. My father had taught me how to do that when I was a teenager. Comforted by the thought, I clambered into the cockpit clutching a packet of biscuits that had fallen from the galley locker.

'Good thinking!' Tom's strained face lit up. 'I'm starving, aren't you?' Food was the last thing on my mind but I nodded in agreement.

'It's very odd. That light has disappeared. I hope nothing awful has happened.' Tom's words echoed my earlier thoughts. He must have realised how scared I felt because he removed his hand from the helm momentarily and squeezed my shoulder.

'We've probably reached the spot where I first saw the light. Take the binoculars and see what you can from the foredeck,' he ordered. 'You may get a clearer view from there.'

I crawled along the deck, clipping and unclipping my safety harness to the lifelines as I moved towards the bow. The pitching motion seemed to be diminishing but the wind had set up a weird whine in the shrouds –

the cables supporting the mast – and the rushing sea seemed very close. I braced myself against the guard rails and scanned the horizon. It was inky dark. With no visible stars and the moon blotted by cloud cover, I could see nothing ahead.

But I could hear an eerie sound. It was the mournful clang of a buoy, warning of rocks in the vicinity. I tried to shout back at Tom but the wind whipped my words away. Fear clutched my stomach. I would have to crawl back along the heaving deck to tell him. By then it might be too late.

As I scrambled into the cockpit I heard a frightening roar. The headsail had split from head to foot and was flapping furiously in the wind, causing the boat to lose power and slow our forward motion. Then a stab of lightning illuminated sea and sky like a powerful searchlight.

Less than a quarter of a mile away, a twin-masted schooner travelling away from us was dipping and riding the waves like a fairground carousel horse. For a moment the light was so bright that even from a distance I could see her name: *Firefly*.

'Over there!' I cried. But Tom was busy releasing the jib sheet and gathering in the sail's torn remnants.

'Shouldn't have had so much canvas up,' he said calmly. 'I'll drop the mainsail and hove-to while this nonsense blows over. We don't want to get near any rocks.'

Hove-to meant angling the boat against the wind and waves, avoiding forward pressure and stopping it dead in its tracks. Another trick my father had demonstrated when I was young but not one I'd ever had cause to repeat. Until now.

'What about the other boat?'

'They've stopped signalling so maybe they've got themselves out of trouble. Anyway, we can't catch up with them now this jib has split and we've lost power. They're belting along like a train.'

For a moment I wondered if his earlier instruction to move along the pitching foredeck with the binoculars had simply been to test my nerve. Dismissing the notion as idiotic, I volunteered to make supper.

It was cosy down below and reasonably stable now we were hove-to. I emptied cans of stew and vegetables into a saucepan and heated it on the stove. On land, I'd never dream of eating such a dog's dinner but at sea the meal tasted like the finest cuisine.

Over supper we planned our time in the Scillies. Tom wanted to enjoy some good, long walks while I was keen to do a bit of bird-watching. We also pondered where best to stock up on supplies for the return journey. When I asked if we would need to visit a chandlery to replace the jib he told me there was no need as he had a spare headsail stowed in the yacht's forepeak.

Every so often Tom removed the hatch and climbed the companionway to check all was well on deck. As the evening wore on, he reported that the wind and rain were easing. Emboldened by relief that the storm was abating, I expressed my admiration for the unruffled way he'd handled what could have been a potentially disastrous situation. In turn he complimented me on keeping calm in unexpectedly testing circumstances. I felt the experience had drawn us together in a more profound way than anything that could have happened on land.

Once the storm had blown through completely we altered course again and headed for the Scillies, taking it in turns to steer the boat or grab a few hours' sleep. Dawn ushered in a cloudless, blue sky and calm seas although the shipping forecast warned of more rain to come later in the day.

The remainder of the passage passed uneventfully and some twenty-eight hours after leaving Plymouth we sailed slowly up the channel between the islands of Tresco and St. Martins. It was a great relief to see land again although I refrained from saying so out loud. Then we dropped anchor and Tom pumped up the inflatable to row ashore.

Two burly fishermen gave us a hand beaching the dinghy on Tresco.

'Anywhere we can get a drink?' asked Tom, his face drawn with exhaustion.

The younger man nodded. 'Over those rocks. The New Inn's just along the path.'

'Could do with a pint myself,' grunted his mate. 'Where've you come from?'

'Plymouth,' replied Tom. 'Weather was foul. The elements threw pretty much everything they could at us.'

'Surprised the lifeboat wasn't called out. A boat got into trouble last night. Heard it on the VHF. See anything out there?'

'I thought I saw an SOS,' replied Tom. 'We headed in her direction to see if we could help. Then she changed course and seemed okay as she'd stopped signalling. It was a yacht called - '

'*Firefly*,' I chipped in, refusing to allow the conversation to turn into a man-to-man sailing yarn. I'd seen the name clearly marked on her stern during those incredibly bright flashes of lightning and had told Tom over supper when we were hove-to.

'Nah, that weren't it,' said the older chap. 'It was *Seaspray*.'

He turned towards me and stared uncomfortably hard. 'A bad time for sailing round here this late in October. A young couple got caught out last year. We told them a storm was brewin' but they wouldn't listen. Said they were in a hurry to reach Falmouth.'

'What happened?' I asked.

'Sank just off the Lizard. The lifeboat put out when they saw her flares but she went down before they reached her. The bodies came ashore next day.'

I shivered, aghast. That could have been us, I thought. Luckily, Tom's clear thinking and calm reactions had kept us safe. I wondered how experienced the other couple had been. Were they novices or did they just take a silly risk?

'This boat that got into trouble last night... *Seaspray*...what was her position when she put out the call?' asked Tom.

The fisherman rubbed his chin. '48 north 5 west, I think they said.'

'Roughly where we were last night before we tacked and headed inshore to look for her,' said Tom. 'That was a close shave. The eye of the gale must have passed south of us while we were lying hove-to, tucked in nearer the coast. *Seaspray* must have hit the worst of it.'

I stared at him while the implications of what he was saying sank slowly into my tired brain.

'You mean we were lured out of danger?'

'In effect,' said Tom. 'Heading inshore saved us from being caught out like that poor couple last year.'

My mind reeled. I could clearly picture what I'd seen in the night. The schooner romping through the waves heading away from us. Those vivid flashes of illumination. The name clearly visible on the stern: *Firefly*.

All my senses had been on high alert during the storm. There was no way I had confused the yacht's name with *Seaspray*. The schooner I'd seen at a distance couldn't have been the one we'd changed course to help then, could it? Unless...

I tuned back into the conversation. 'That's such a tragic story – lost at sea,' said Tom. "Getting into trouble in a storm is every sailor's worst fear. That poor couple must have been terrified.'

Then he frowned, as if wrestling with a puzzling thought. 'What did you say their yacht was called?'

His question was never answered. A fierce downpour prompted the fishermen to hurry off in the direction of The New Inn, leaving us alone on the beach.

Standing there in the rain I felt Tom's arms encircle my shoulders, pulling me close and cherishing me. My spirits soared. After all the drama of the previous night it felt like an absolution.

I was tempted to voice the weird idea fizzing in my mind but remained silent, thinking Tom would laugh at me.

Ghostly schooner or trick of the light, I didn't care. In that moment what mattered more was the kindred spirit I had found at sea.

HYDROCEPHALUS

JAMIE CHIPPERFIELD

S ir Gerald Dungworth MP, Secretary of State for the Environment, sat in his wood-panelled Westminster office, waiting for the guillotine to drop.

Sir Gerald had achieved little in the six months since his appointment, other than dining on as many subsidised meals as possible and amassing his parliamentary pension fund. Even the most ardent party loyalist would have had trouble explaining how, exactly, he was serving the people.

Gerald slammed his fist onto the desk, cursing at the air around him. 'Where are the ideas when I need them? I thought Britain was supposed to be a land of innovation? So why am I cursed with nothing but braindead idiots?'

'What did you say, Sir Gerald?' called Sebastian from the adjoining room, before appearing in the doorway.

'Oh, nothing,' moaned Gerald.

'I bring good news,' announced Sebastian, a chief advisor whose only qualification was that he was someone's nephew and whose abilities were even fewer. 'The PM has moved your meeting to tomorrow afternoon.'

Stay of execution, thought Gerald, grimly.

'That doesn't solve my predicament. The PM wants my guts for garters. I need ideas. Good ones. Ones that'll win votes at the next election.'

'I get my best ideas in the shower,' blurted Sebastian without thinking, as per usual.

'How the hell does that help me?'

'I don't know. If everyone had more showers, there'd be more ideas in the world? Does that help? Also, everyone would smell better too.'

'You want me to tell the nation that they should be showering more? No. I don't think so. They already hate us enough without us telling the plebs that they smell.'

Sebastian held up his hands in appeasement. 'All I'm saying is it works for me. I don't know why. But it does. Maybe it's the vitamins in the water or something.'

'There's no vitamins in the... Hang on a minute, who's been telling you there are... *vitamins*... in the water.'

'Oh, I spent an enlightening afternoon in a yurt at Glasto last year with some monks calling themselves the guardians of the fountain of knowledge. Or something like that? They seemed to really know what they were talking about. And it definitely wasn't just the special tea.'

Something clicked in Gerald's head. Something desperate. 'Actually, you might have something there. Get researching, man. I want potential action plans by end of day. Something. Anything.'

'I think I've still got the chief's mobile number. And it definitely wasn't a cult...'

***

Sharon, Shazza to her friends, was experiencing her first day as an apprentice at the local water treatment plant. Never before had she been so bored. She was, quite literally, bored shitless.

'...and over here is where we process the solid matter,' continued her supervisor, seemingly just as bored.

So uninterested was Sharon that her mind had begun to wander, and instead of paying attention to the orientation tour, found only questions of an existential nature.

Is this really it? The rest of my life? How did it come to this? They told us we could be anything we wanted. Astronauts. Ballerinas. Olympic show jumpers. Adulthood was supposed to be fun and freedom. Not this?

But then, through the creaking maze of pipes, tanks and valves, she spotted a sight so incongruous and absurd that it dragged her from her reverie. She blinked. Hard. Several times. Just in case the local fumes were causing her to hallucinate.

'Keith? I'm not imagining that... am I?'

Keith stopped mid-flow, confused, and examined the area she was pointing at.

At the very edge of the plant was a scene pulled straight from a children's storybook. Just beyond the final solids tank stood a small, thatched-roof wicker hut, smoke puffing gently from its chimney.

'Oh that,' replied Keith, dismissively. 'New orders from head office. Bunch of druids brought in from Suffolk. Keep to themselves mostly.' He shrugged, as if it was a completely normal thing to say.

'Druids? Working here?'

Keith shrugged again.

'What do they do all day? What could they possibly do in a place like this?'

Keith shrugged for a third time, it appeared to be a habit. 'If it came from the higher ups, someone must know what it's all about.'

'So, you don't know? asked Sharon, incredulous. 'Have you not thought to ask about the sudden appearance of druids in your workplace?'

Keith paused, his head tilting thoughtfully towards the sky, the signs of deep concentration etched across his face. He froze where he stood, but his mind kept churning. The struggle was clear to see as he strained for an epiphany that remained just out of reach. Then his mouth fell open and his gaze drifted back to Sharon, who imagined for a moment that the secrets of the universe were about to spill forth. But Keith simply glanced at his watch, and the realisation cruelly vanished into the aether.

'Oh bugger,' cried Keith. 'Is that really the time? We need get this induction tour moving or I'm going to miss my lunch! That bloody Steve is not getting my sausage roll. Not again.'

He set off again at a blistering pace. She sighed wearily and trotted after him, any thoughts of druids soon replaced with the workings of filtration tanks and other mundane things.

***

'It's only me Dad,' called Georgia as she let herself in.

'I've got your paper,' she continued, closing the front door and pocketing the spare keys to her father's bungalow. 'Did you want me to do your lunch?'

Georgia paused to rifle through her father's post just in case something important had lain neglected on the hall carpet. She mumbled to herself as she thumbed through the pile of letters, announcing the nature of each one purely out of habit. Satisfied there was nothing pressing, she left the pile on the desk in the hall. Georgia had yet to notice that there had been no reply from her father.

Georgia walked into the open plan kitchen-living area and immediately headed for the fridge. 'The boys send their love. They're looking forward to seeing you Sunday, if you're still up to it,' she called as she opened the fridge. 'I see you don't need anything from the shop. Do you want anything done while I'm here?'

A surge of fear churned her stomach as her father's failure to respond finally registered. She turned to examine the living area and noticed first his empty armchair, then both his zimmerframe and his walking stick. The only sign of any recent presence was a half-drunk glass of water on the table beside his armchair.

A sudden *clang* shattered the silence, followed by a more subtle metallic rattle. Georgia's heart pounded as she floundered in a rising tide of panic.

The rattle and scrape of metal continued as Georgia tried frantically to track down the source of the noise, visions of her father bruised and bleeding on the ground adding to her torment. She wished she hadn't watched so many episodes of *Casualty*.

In the garden, Georgia was greeted with the sight of her father, her scrawny-limbed, grey-haired, eighty-year-old father, climbing onto the roof of his bungalow.

'Dad!' shouted Georgia nervously, wary of spooking him. 'What are you doing up there?'

Henry had propped his ladder against the garden shed adjacent to the flat-roofed section of his bungalow, and to his daughter's astonishment, ascended the ladder with a sure-footedness she'd never seen before.

'One second, love,' called Henry, planting a frail, outstretched hand onto the flat of the roof.

'What on earth are you doing, Dad?' Georgia implored, as her facade of calm began to crumble. Henry did not reply, instead precariously placing one knee on the roof, with only a hand and a tiptoe still in contact with the ladder. 'Dad! Come down! You've never been up on the roof! Ever! What about your vertigo?'

'Don't worry love, I just need to sort out this leaky roof,' he replied, oblivious to his situation.

'With what? You're not even a roofer!'

And then, with one last Olympian push, Henry had both feet on the roof, for the first time in his life. With an unbridled sense of achievement spreading across his face, he drew himself up and stood proudly with hands on hips. Georgia looked up at her father, a silhouette of Superman now standing on the bungalow roof, and felt both terror and amazement in equal measure.

'Good lord! I can see the whole neighbourhood from up here. I can see fields! And look! There's the tree where I first kissed your mother. And there's the church where we got married. And there's...and there's...' his voice trailed off as tears filled his eyes.

'Oh Dad. I know. I know. Come down now please and I'll make you a cup of tea.'

Henry finally looked down at his worried daughter and suddenly seemed to forget what had brought him up there in the first place.

'I...' started Henry, but it was at that very moment that his vertigo returned. It began as a wobble of the knees. A sway of the body. No longer did he seem quite so upright. 'Oh my,' cried Henry as he finally realised his predicament.

He began to kneel so that he could climb back down, but the weight of his body (and of the situation) on his eighty-year-old knees was too much to bear. They gave way and Henry lurched violently over the precipice. He tried to save himself from the inevitable, hands grasping for the ladder, for a handhold, for anything, and in doing so spun himself as he tumbled through the air in the direction of his shed. At least it was a shorter drop than to the ground.

But the shed roof, like his knees, immediately gave way beneath him and he plummeted straight through it. Then, one by one, the walls of the shed fell in on him.

Georgia witnessed all this in silent horror, experiencing it in slow motion. It seemed to last a lifetime. The ensuing silence stretching even longer.

A creak of wood. The crunch of shifting rubble.

'I'm ok,' called Henry weakly.

'Dad! I'm coming! I'm coming!' shouted Georgia, rushing toward the ruined shed, dialling for an ambulance.

***

Mary sighed mournfully at the aftermath of the dinner she had cooked for her husband. The scratched dining table and the tired kitchen were of little comfort at the end of a long day, even less so when she contemplated the cleaning that awaited her.

She cleared the table first, dutifully transferring dirty dishes to the sink until only her husband's newspaper remained. That day's headline stared up at her. *Scientists Baffled At Nationwide Spike In IQ.*

'Utter nonsense,' muttered Mary, and promptly dropped it in the recycling.

Mary collected the remaining pots and pans scattered around the kitchen and added them to the sink with a resounding splosh. She took one look at the mound of washing up that had formed, a veritable iceberg of Teflon and china cresting above the soap-frothed waterline, and sighed. A solitary thirty minutes of joyless washing and drying awaited her, with nothing but the silence of her kitchen to keep her company.

Before she plunged her hands into the water, Mary poked her head around the corner into the adjoining living room. The room was dark but for the unnatural glow of the flatscreen TV mounted on the wall. Caught in its light was the shape of her husband, a slob of a man, as he slavishly stared at the screen while scratching his ample belly. *So you can multitask when you want to*, thought Mary bitterly. She could have said it out loud and it would have gone unnoticed. Trevor was always dead to the world while *Police Interceptors Uncut XL* was on. It was his favourite program, and God forbid anything should interrupt it.

Mary had been about to return to her washing up when she saw the pair of tea-stained Sports Direct mugs by her husband's feet. He had eight of the damn things. A full matching set for company, as he put it, plus spares. They took up an entire shelf. And while Mary considered the plates inherited from her grandmother to be their best china, delicate plates of white and blue porcelain that her grandmother had saved for a year to purchase, it was those oversized, mass-produced mugs that were Trevor's chosen pride and joy. *You wash them up, you lazy bastard*, thought Mary.

Mary returned to the kitchen and braced herself for another evening at the sink. She plunged her hands in the warm, foamy water, and reached for the first plate. But she was interrupted by a peculiar sensation that fell upon her with all the force of a ten-foot wave. She felt... strange. Indescribably so. Like nothing she'd ever experienced. But then she noticed a sudden surge of new energy. She was revived. Reborn. A new woman. And with it came a flood of thoughts and ideas, many of which she should not have been entertaining.

Then her attention returned to the sink. To her hands.

She had unconsciously picked up the carving knife.

She did not put it down.

***

Detective Inspector Brown leaned against the bonnet of his car, waiting for his colleague to return from the coffee run. There was always a queue. It was always a long wait, but Brown came prepared and proceeded to unfurl his newspaper.

But DI Wells emerged from the coffee shop far sooner than expected.

'One cappuccino, extra sprinkles,' announced Wells, as he handed it over.

Brown took it with a puzzled expression. 'That was quicker than usual.'

'Yeah, it's practically empty in there today.'

'Wait, where's your coffee?'

Wells answered by pulling a bottle of mineral water from his pocket.

'What's this nonsense? Water? You detoxing or something?' asked Brown.

'You know what they say, happy wife, happy life,' replied Wells.

Brown sipped at his coffee thoughtfully.

Wells unscrewed his bottle of water and pointed at his partner's newspaper. '*Nationwide spike in IQ*? If you say so.'

'I swear something weird is going on at the moment. Look at this one, a couple of pages in. *Rising crime rate threat to public*.'

'It's not surprising the papers have noticed.'

'Exactly. It's bloody everywhere. The sudden increase in domestic incidents. More crimes perpetrated by the middle and upper classes. More crimes involving swimming pools and hot tubs. Not to mention the current violence in the wellness community. As I said, something really weird is going on.'

'Too true,' agreed Wells.

'And there's the issue of the CPS. I hear it's like every brief is suddenly KC or something. They just can't get convictions to stick anymore.'

'Strange times indeed.'

Wells finally sipped his mineral water, pondering what such omens could possibly mean. He'd been about to take another sip when he found himself struck by an unseen force. This was no ordinary, single point-of-impact type event. Wells knew how that felt from the thankfully few times he had been shot or stabbed. This was something else entirely. Something that surged through one's being as if struck by lightning, lightning that might have come from Zeus himself.

Brown was alerted by the sudden jolt of his partner. 'You alright there, mate?'

Wells was silent, frozen to the spot.

'You okay?' asked Brown again, increasingly concerned. Strokes were not unheard of in their profession. The stress of the job took its toll.

Wells murmured something weak and inaudible.

'What was that?'

But then Wells found his voice. 'OF COURSE! THE JOHNSON CASE! IT WAS THE KOI CARP ALL ALONG!'

'What?' asked a clueless Brown,

'THE JOHNSON CASE! THE JOHNSON CASE!' Repeated Wells, continuing to shout. 'IT WAS THE KOI CARP!'

'Slow down man! You're not making any sense.'

But Wells did the exact opposite of slowing down. He launched himself from the bonnet and bolted for the driver's-side door, keys in hand, and had the engine revving within a heartbeat. Brown barely had time to throw himself into the passenger seat before the car was hurtling down the street, in search of guilty koi carp.

***

Freya was never happier than when she was roaming the countryside. Come rain or shine she could be found wandering the fields and woodland around her cottage like some figure from rural folklore. She firmly believed there was no greater joy in life than the scent of freshly wet earth, rising as petrichor into the air, and that far too many people spent their lives trying to escape the rain. It was foolish. You simply cannot escape water. Water is the source of all life. Water is life.

But Freya wandered with purpose that afternoon. She was on a mission.

She adored the countryside in its entirety, but what she truly loved were its rivers. Most of her childhood memories revolved around rivers, hours spent happily splashing in the shallows with her parents and siblings, which evolved into a love of wild swimming in her youth and early adulthood. Sadly, those days were well behind her, she was no longer so active, but she could accept such inevitability. The ravages of time were a natural part of life. What she could not accept was the *unnatural*.

Freya marched down the hedgerow-lined footpath with an air of militant officiousness, the river not yet in sight. Cows mooed contently from the adjoining fields, out of sight, oblivious to the state of the world in which they found themselves. Freya, however, was far from oblivious. She had taken it upon herself to be the canary in the coal mine. A self-appointed guardian of the countryside. A lone warden against utter ruination. The last line of defence.

As always, she smelled the river before she saw it, and her nose wrinkled in response. She crested a rise and the path before her opened onto a sloping riverbank. A gaping wound meandering through otherwise green and pleasant countryside. The river's waters were brown and foul, a stain on both the landscape and Freya's precious memories. Her heart bled at the sight of it, not only for herself, but for all the life that depended on this vital habitat. While Freya could choose not to swim in those vile waters, the same could not be said for the creatures that had no choice but to try to live in it. She regularly found dead fish washed up on the riverbank, their small, fragile bodies conspicuously intact.

Freya continued along the riverside path, looking for a spot where the bank wasn't so steep. Stones littered the river beside her, large and dark, like the backs of monsters rising from the murky deep. Each one as slick as polished gemstones, coated not only in river water, but in a slime of synthetic chemicals.

The slope of the riverbank eventually softened and Freya stepped from the path and carefully eased herself down toward the water's edge and then onto her knees, making sure that she did not touch the water. She felt the damp, soft earth through her jeans. She rummaged through her messenger bag, feeling for the familiar shape of her water monitoring equipment. A jar and a sensor. So much could be achieved with so little.

With a gloved hand, Freya scooped a jar of water from the river and held it up to the light. The murky, faecal-coloured contents spoke for themselves. She dropped in the sensor, tightened the cap and then set down the sealed jar. Freya sighed as she pulled her smartphone from her pocket and activated the app connected to the sensor, waiting for the results to appear on screen. She surveyed the river as she allowed the equipment to do its work. She knew what to expect, and it wasn't a miracle. A gradual decline was the best she could hope for.

The results flashed up on screen. Freya's eyebrow arched in response.

All the usual suspects were present. Chemical runoff from the local farms. Raw sewage dumped by water companies upstream. Microplastics and other man-made waste discarded by a negligent population. But now there were words she had not seen before. *Unknown contaminant*. In significant quantities.

Freya collected the spare jar and sensor from her bag and repeated the process, collecting another sample from further along the flattened riverbank. The result was identical.

She gathered up her things and headed back with purpose. 'I need to report this. I need to tell someone,' she muttered to herself repeatedly.

From nowhere, she felt a sudden resolve swell within her, a vindication that her stewardship of the waterways really meant something. Eager to report her findings, she picked up the pace and hurried home.

***

'Wake up guys,' said Cedric, his face lit by the glow of his iPhone in the early morning gloom 'The gig's up. We're in the papers.'

Groggy, semi-asleep groans came from the other two hammocks.

'WAKE. UP.' Reiterated Cedric.

Balthasar yawned in response, stirring at last. 'We heard you the first time.'

'Oh well, fun while it lasted,' murmured Zephyr from the other hammock, not bothering to move.

'Come on. Up you get,' urged Cedric. 'We need to slip away while it's still dark.'

Zephyr dangled his legs over the side of his hammock. 'I'm going to miss these consultancy fees.'

'I hate these corporate gigs,' said Balthasar, also beginning to rouse himself.

'It made a change from playing Gandalf for yet another Lord Of The Rings themed wedding,' said Zephyr.

'Again,' added Balthasar.

'And again,' said Zephyr.

'It did pay the bills for a few months, though,' said Balthasar.

'Speak for yourself,' replied Zephyr. 'Work to live, not live to work, I say. All this water money means I'm finally going on my grand tour of the ley lines.'

'I might actually get to Stonehenge for the solstice, for once,' said Balthasar.

'That's all very nice,' interjected Cedric. 'But I'm not seeing much movement here.'

'Alright Merlin, keep your beard on,' replied Balthasar. 'It's early. TOO EARLY.'

'Not too early for a witch hunt. Or in this case, a druid hunt.'

'Calm down, it's not the seventeenth century anymore. Nobody knows what we're up to.'

'They do. Or near enough. They *know* that something is in the water. And they will *know* where it came from. The papers are already rallying the pitchforks by calling it bioterrorism. We can't be complacent about this.'

'Typical,' spat Zephyr vehemently, as he sat up. 'The government asked for our help. Demanded it, for the good of the nation. It was them! THEM! They started all this, but we'll be the ones investigated and made into scapegoats.'

'We warned them, what they were unleashing,' added Cedric, solemnly. 'We told them the magic wasn't perfect, nor the means of delivery. The human mind behaves strangely enough without the interference of magic. There was no guarantee that inspiration sorcery would lead to good ideas.'

'And yet they demanded it anyway.'

The three druids lingered in the silence, complicit in all that had taken place.

'Thank goodness they didn't want to know where the ideas really came from,' said Balthasar.

'I don't think they would have agreed to this scheme had they known,' replied Zephyr.

'And then we'd never have been paid.'

'They obviously have never read Sweeney Todd,' added Cedric. 'Never ask what's in the pies.'

***

Sir Gerald Dungworth MP, Secretary of State for the Environment, sat in his wood-panelled Westminster office, waiting for the guillotine to drop. Again. Only this time the guillotine had already begun to fall.

Everything was gone, or would be by the end of the day. His cabinet position. His office. His status. Even Sebastian had abandoned him, the very person who had made the suggestion, whisked away by his influential uncle before the shit well and truly hit the fan.

If being demoted to irrelevance wasn't bad enough, Sir Gerald was now such a stain on the party that he was being leant on to resign from parliament. He was faced with the prospect that the party, *his party*, would rather fight a mid-term by-election – and lose – than allow him to fester on the back benches for the next eighteen months.

They were even threatening to take back his knighthood.

The scandal had been dubbed Watergate, but they remembered that the name was already taken, and Druidgate became the colloquialism of choice for this debacle. *His* debacle, as all of Westminster kept reminding him.

When the news broke, the water companies were initially held responsible. But blame is an ever-flowing river, one whose current only flows upstream. It did not take long for the water executives to point the finger at those who had instructed them to hire the druids in the first place. And from there it was but a short paddle to the desk of Sir Gerald himself. The Prime Minister couldn't amputate him fast enough. Allowing bioterrorists potential access to national infrastructure will have that affect.

'There's nothing else for it,' huffed Sir Gerald to the empty room. 'I might as well, I suppose.'

He opened a drawer and placed the bottle of water on the desk in front of him. It was, after all, the only honourable thing to do. He could only hope, despite the well-documented risks, ideas would follow.

CAVERNOUS AND ERUDITE

JASON COBLEY

Cavernous and erudite, the ceiling of the Library Chapel shimmered with words carved from watery graves. It sang with green, echoed with deep blue, and murmured a white shadow on the shelves that lined the walls.

Deilen's jaw was slack in awe. Then, momentarily aware, he clenched his teeth. Books filled the shelves that towered and arched upwards, forever upwards, to the iridescent ceiling. There was no visible way to climb the shelves or call the books down, their embossed spines so tantalisingly out of reach. He stood on the carpet, his boots having tracked in flakes of dry mud, feeling out of place.

The Librarian cleared her throat. 'Can I be of assistance, sir?' she said.

Deilen's attention shifted towards the woman seated at the desk that faced him. In the centre of the octagonal room, it was a mahogany semi-circle behind which she waited. Her hand was poised over the blank pages of a leatherbound journal, the pen in her fingers sparkling with light from within.

'Oh, hello. I don't know.' Deilen fumbled for words. 'I don't actually know why I'm here.'

'Indeed?' She nodded, the tightly arranged sculpture of her hair swaying slightly. Her gown recalled Regency design, dark rose silk spilling effortlessly either side of her chair. She touched her throat with her fingertips as Deilen stepped closer.

'No, sorry,' he said, blushing.

'Perhaps I can help you there. Take a seat.' She gestured to the chair that was his side of the desk, the wave of her hand like gossamer.

Deilen sat, loosening the buttons on his leather peacoat. As he relaxed, the bookcases seemed to sag and sigh with him. Startled, his eyes darted, trying to spot where the sound was coming from.

'Never mind them,' said the Librarian. 'Sentient bookcases are rather too fond of pathetic fallacy. Don't get them started on poems. That's worse. I had to referee an argument between the literary criticism section and the Philip Larkin shelves on the correct pacing of trochaic rhythm the other day. It went on for hours.'

The Librarian's hands moved fluidly, diaphanous wisps of fingers painting the air with whispers. Deilen was mesmerised by them until he was drawn to her serious face once more. 'Sorry,' he repeated.

'No need. Now to business. Can I ask your name, sir?'

He knew that much. 'Deilen,' he said.

'Ah,' she replied, writing it down. 'Welsh for "leaf", I believe, How can we help you today at the Library Chapel, Mister Deilen?'

'Just Deilen.'

'Lovely. Very poetic. I love Welsh literature. Mabinogion is a lovely young man. Anyway. How can we help?'

'I don't know. I mean, the only thing I remember is standing here on the carpet. My boots are a bit muddy, I'm afraid, and I've got my coat on, so I'm guessing I walked here, but...' He furrowed his brow and gestured hesitantly, as if choosing a piece to place in the centre of a jigsaw puzzle.

'You remember nothing else?'

'That's right.' He ran his hands over his stubble and through his lank black hair, as if trying to wipe away the bewilderment.

'I understand.'

'I wish I did.'

'Look around you,' she said, gesturing mistily in the direction of the bookshelves that rose up around them like giant redwood trees. 'What do you see?'

'Books.'

She leaned across the desk, within whispering distance of his ear. Her breath was like petrichor. 'What do you hear?'

'I hadn't noticed before. Voices... muttering... just about audible... I can't quite make them out. And maybe music... hesitant... discordant... like jazz,' he replied. He found his words leading his thinking, uttering ahead of him, almost as if they had their own life.

'You're hearing the books. In the highest reaches, the classics rub shoulders and talk philosophy. The music you're hearing is literary fiction. They're having the best time up there, improvising and teasing the poetry enclave. Commercial fiction is all over the place. We give each genre their own chamber, so they can do their thing in peace. I only go into the romance fiction corridor to dust. They're so self-involved, it's a shame.'

Deilen nodded in wonder. 'This is the strangest library I've ever been in,' he said, then paused. 'Actually, I think it's the first library I've ever been in.'

The Librarian floated around the desk and offered Deilen her hand. He took it and rose from the chair. Her palm was cool and faintly exciting to the touch. 'Come with me,' she said, and led him through a gap in the shelves that parted like a tissue-thin curtain.

They descended a flight of stairs, the walls recessed with shelves holding old, dog-eared paperbacks that fluttered like moths when Deilen passed them. One of them sniggered, causing Deilen to flinch.

'Take no notice. They're the dirty books. Even though most of them are electronic these days, they still arrive here all grubby and sticky. There's too many of them to ignore but no one really wants to file them, so they find their own little corners and passageways to lurk in. Honestly, I think they're happier like that,' said the Librarian as she pondered whether to go right or left at the foot of the staircase.

She chose left. 'Ah, here we are,' she sighed, spinning into another vast room that matched the one they left, except this time the air seemed to hang with heaviness, careworn and still.

Deilen took in the differences. 'The books. There are thousands, maybe millions. I can't see where they end,' he said, pointing to the vanishing point far above. 'But they're quiet. And plain. They all look the same, sort of beige. No writing on the spines, as far as I can see.'

'Oh, you'll see when you get closer. If we had gone in the other direction, we would be in the Acre of Unfinished Novels, the ones where the authors died before they could complete them. You might have come across The Mystery of Edwin Drood wandering about. He can't rest, you see, because people who aren't Dickens keep thinking about him and trying to finish him, if only in their heads. He broods on it quite a bit. So moody! Jane Austen's Sanditon gets really annoyed with him. She hit him once. With an imaginary shovel she got from Mark Twain's Mysterious Stranger. Unfinished novels can be so... unpredictable.'

'I daresay.'

The Librarian spread her arms wide, perspiring glitter that flew towards Deilen. He blushed. Undeterred, she pirouetted and laughed. 'You see all these plain beige books? They're not like that inside, you know. Well, some of them are, but everyone has their place here.'

'What sort of books are they?'

'Oh, you see, Deilen, it's very important you understand this. They are the Forgotten Folios. They're the books that busy housewives write but never have the courage to try to get published. They're the books that tortured geniuses scrawl with blood and ink and, with self-loathing, consign to the fire before anyone can read them. They're the novels that the writers, weighed down with rejection and criticism, delete from their computers, convinced that they'll never be good enough. Sometimes they're right, you know, but so many other times…' she said, trailing off.

Deilen looked down at his hands. His palms were lined with manual labour, his nails scored with the honesty of toil. Yet somehow, they also seemed fragile, like dry parchment. 'I think I know what you're telling me.'

'Do you?' She was beside him again and then swept around his back, soft and limpid.

'Yes, I think so. Did I… write one of these books? Am I… could I be… an author?' There was a hint of disgust in the uplift at the end of his sentence.

The Librarian laughed so much that tiny curls of apricot perfume escaped her hair and twirled away to the atrium above. 'Not quite,' she managed to say, composing herself.

'What then? Why am I here?'

She straightened, business-like again. Tenderly, she spoke, her eyes on his, her hand resting gently on his tight knuckles. 'You are here not because you wrote a book. You *are* a book.'

'Come again?'

'More accurately, you're the visual manifestation of an idea, the personification of a novel. Don't worry. Everyone is like this when they orientate. We find it helps. You've spent so much time coming alive in someone's head that, when you arrive here, you're so confused you don't know what you are.'

'Oh.'

'You don't seem shocked.'

'Should I be? I mean, now I think about it, it makes sense. It feels like I didn't exist until I was gazing up at that first ceiling of books.' A playful look came into his eye. 'Was I any good?'

'That's the thing, you see. You probably were. Or you would have been. Except your author deleted you. He'd finished you, every word. But he had a crisis of confidence and wiped the whole thing. The whole you. But, you see, ideas don't die. Not really. They end up here. There's a space for you on the shelves over there.'

'All beige and basic? No thank you! I want to go back. I bet I could be an amazing book.' Deilen surprised himself by his reaction. He did not know it yet, but this was his first experience of fear. 'Why was I deleted?'

The Librarian flittered around him, wafting her ephemeral arms, as if fanning the information from his pheromones. She inhaled deeply, then nodded as if affirming understanding. Taking a seat at the central desk, she motioned for Deilen to join her. He sat on the chair opposite her.

'Different desk, but we're back where we started,' he said. 'No further forward.'

'I wouldn't say that. I've picked up a few things... excuse me...' she said, and sneezed. Tiny blossoms flurried through the air from her nose. She continued, 'Oops, sorry. Your synopsis made me a little sneezy'.

'My synopsis?'

'Yes.' She hesitated. 'I found it somewhat irritable. It seems it was rejected by agents because it lacks the elements needed for commercial success in a crowded market.'

'Oh. But that's... what, just a summary of me? What would have to change?'

'Well... what genre are you?'

Deilen looked down at his clothes: leather peacoat, stylish boots, scarf. 'I don't know. Historical fiction?'

'Those tend to sell if they're also a romance, preferably written by a woman for a female audience. Or set in a concentration camp purporting to be a true story. I don't think it's that. You don't look like a cosy comedy detective story set in a sleepy English village either.'

'Does it make a difference who wrote me?'

'Well, you're obviously not written by a celebrity. Or you'd have definitely been published.'

Deilen stood. Arms behind his back, he paced the carpet, looking up at the skyscraping shelves. A shaft of light from above hit one of the shelves, several feet above his head. 'What's wrong with me, anyway? As far as I can work out – it's coming back to me now – I have a good plot. Revenge. Action. Character quirks. Interesting central character. Wait... I get it now. It's written in the first person. Deilen is the protagonist. It's me. I'm not just *in* the book – I'm the hero of the thing!'

The Librarian looked nervous. She left her seat, floating across the floor to settle beside Deilen. She seemed to him to become more solid, her skin a faint but substantial alabaster. Looking him in the eyes, as if seeing something new, she said, 'This is most irregular. I was mistaken. You're...'

'A character,' he replied with a smirk. 'The ghost of a character wiped from a trashy crime novel. The author was trying to make it more literary. Decided I had to go. The rest of the book is still being written. I can feel it. But he cut me out.' He pursed his lips. Something deep inside him trembled, as if trying to shake itself free.

'Right. This is very unusual, but I believe we do have a storage area in the lower east wing of the Library Chapel, beneath the Chancery of Political Tracts. Let me show you the way. I'm sure you'll be comfortable there.'

His face darkened; his brow creased. He shook his head. He was not going to budge. His eyes darted around the vast chamber, looking for exits. On one side was the enclosed passage from which they came. Across the other side of the desk was an entrance to a similar shadowy corridor. A light breeze came from that end, brushing against his skin. Fixating on that destination, he stepped around the desk.

The Librarian was between Deilen and the exit. She was more solid than ever, her arms folded, a scowl creasing her pearlescent features.

'Let me pass,' Deilen said.

'No,' she replied. 'You will follow me, Deilen'.

'I want to leave. I want to be real again. I want to mean something. I don't want to just be the memory of a character that wasn't good enough. Don't you see?'

All of the softness, all of the misty, weightless butterfly smoothness of the Librarian, hardened in that moment. She stood resolute, her Regency gown transformed into a hessian kimono, a sword sheathed in the belt wrapped around her waist.

The Librarian said, 'I do. I also see why you were deleted. Your author decided against having a murderer as his narrator. You were a first draft. The story has changed. His protagonist is a young female detective on her first job. You are a minor character in the background, a case that is solved early in the story. What stands before me is the rejected first draft. That is all you are. You shall not pass.'

A knife made of polished ivory grew out of Deilen's open palm. Staring at it with amusement, he said, 'Looks like we can both transform ourselves for battle. Is that all this place is? A place to imagine things?'

Brandishing the blade, gripping the handle tightly, Deilen readied to fight. The Librarian drew her sword and took a warrior's stance, her feet planted firmly and steadfast. 'Not really. Every book here was thought up by someone. But I'm the Librarian and I must curate the volumes, protect the content, let nothing escape.'

Nodding towards the exit, Deilen said, 'What if I do, though? What's through there?'

The Librarian looked over her shoulder at the doorway. As Deilen focused on it, the doorframe shimmered, grey at the edges, growing darker at the centre. Wherever it led, it was not simply another corridor or staircase. He could smell the air seeping through, full of ozone and eddying wind. She blocked his path with her sword as he stepped forward. He stopped and adjusted his grip around the knife. Knuckles white, it was as if his hand was resisting his command to strike, stab or slash.

'To the best of my knowledge, I've never used a knife,' he said. 'I've never killed anyone. Yet, you said I was written as a murderer.'

'Perhaps your author gave you the motivation, but never wrote the actual act. It's just in your synopsis,' she replied, beginning to relax.

'What if that doorway leads into the world?'

'No one knows. Even if it does, you're as ephemeral as me. You won't suddenly manifest as a person, walking down the street, catching the bus, eating pizza, bullying people on your phone. You're the ghost of an idea, that's all.'

'Maybe I'll find another book. Maybe I can turn up in another story, hide in there as another character. Maybe that's how I can survive.' He was excited by the idea.

Softening, the Librarian was pleading. 'No, please don't. You could... you could stay with me; help maintain the shelves. It's a beautiful eternity. Really, it is, but sometimes it can be a lonely existence.' With a flourish, her sword shivered into the folds of her clothes, the kimono shifting back into a humble Regency gown. Once again, she stood before him as she was when he met her.

Deilen willed his knife into a single red rose, the morning dew still fresh on its petals. With a bow, he presented it to the Librarian. Blushing, she accepted the gift. Holding the flower to her nose, she inhaled the fragrance as she allowed him to step past her. Before he crossed the threshold, he paused and said, 'Maybe I'll turn over a new leaf.'

The darkness of the portal swallowed his form and all the light that surrounded him. With a slam, the shadows became a door, and closed. The Librarian watched the closed door wistfully. Although she knew instinctively that it would never open again, she waited. It may have been minutes or millennia that she waited; time worked differently in the Library Chapel. After what may have been hours or eons, she turned away, floated up to the shaft of light that illuminated one of the shelves, and began rearranging the order of the books. Back to work.

Pages turned.

Deilen, whose name was the Welsh word for 'leaf', blinked at the brightness of the blankness that surrounded him. He felt the words start to form, then...

But that's another story.

THE ELEMENTS OF JAZZ

A.B. KYAZZE

Georgia's head ached and she didn't know if it was last night's vodka or slamming her forehead against the wall when she'd realised what she had done. Her sax sat wounded in its case. She couldn't face it. Couldn't pull herself out of bed to assess the damage. She didn't think it was salvageable, and where would that leave her?

Hating herself, hating her life at that moment, she lay in bed and couldn't move. It hurt to think. Hurt to blink. Couldn't move her eyes away from the cracked ceiling where her housemate had let the bathtub overflow that time. There was a slip of paper Sellotaped on the wall with words that were supposed to soothe her mind:

The elements of jazz are simple: you just need a voice, a rhythm, and to create the energy between them.

Manu's words stayed with Georgia, even though she hadn't seen her mentor for years. She had typed up a copy and kept it as she moved between bedsits and into the grubby house share in Catford, the only place she could afford. She even thought about getting it as a tattoo, lacing around her biceps like an armband. But when she got to *Tatooooze* on her 18th birthday, she heard a girl screaming and chickened out. She got a small treble clef instead, on the inside of her wrist. Still hurt like hell. But she looks at it most days and thinks of Manu.

Voice, rhythm, and energy. People always assume that when you talk about 'voice' it has to be a singer, but Georgia was never a singer. People laughed at her when she tried, cracked jokes if they thought she was not listening. But voice doesn't have to be a woman or a man. A tenor sax has a sound that soars and dips; it can lead with a solo, or complement the other voices at play.

The rhythm can be any kind of percussion: drums, hand or steel, no matter what. It gives the music its heartbeat, the pulse. Or an acoustic guitar can do it, with the nice rattle of a pick scraping over the strings in the right way. And you can add layers of other instruments, other voices or rhythms, taking turns and improvising. That is the beauty of jazz.

And the fucking heartbreak of it when you can't do it anymore.

It should have been her big night. They had been working up to it for months. The music promoter, Kai, was so kind. He was this Ugandan guy from North London. He said he liked to find new talent and put them on stage in live venues, mixed with his DJ sets, and then set the performers free to play. Kai had a regular gig night the first Thursday of the month in Peckham, just off the train tracks. Georgia knew Peckham, as Manu used to teach out of a squat they had turned into an art collective before it got bulldozed for flats. After that, Manu left London, left music. Never one for social media or texts, he vanished without much of a goodbye.

Georgia had been thinking of Manu last night as she climbed the steps up to the venue in Peckham. It was one of those redesigned places that catered towards the posh, and the price of drinks was insane. However, this was a paid gig, with promotion and everything. They might even gift her a drink. And who knows, maybe an Uber home, instead of the night bus. She had high hopes.

She was performing with Nambi on drums, and arrived before him. Nambi was super-reliable and easy-going, but often on the late side. They had a simple friendship that involved saying yes to as many gigs as possible.

He was eager to please the clientele, whatever they wanted. Georgia was the more prickly member of the duo. It was hard for her to stomach any criticism or suggestions. That was what was so good about this gig. Kai made it clear it was all about inspiration and expression. And to be honest, as she looked around at the audience, this crowd probably would have most of their attention on the food, and their conversations. She wasn't sure if people were here for the music at all, or if it was just her and Nambi. They'd get paid either way, so there was a real freedom in that.

The night started out well. Kai played chilled soul music on vinyl while the diners took their seats and ordered their meals. The lighting was low, but Georgia couldn't read music so that was no problem. She felt a little under dressed compared to some of these people. The customers obviously had money. A lot of silver and gold and full, pumped-up lips.

Georgia didn't wear any makeup. What was the point? Her skin was so pale and freckled you couldn't do anything about it. Sometimes a bit of mascara, to draw people's eyes away from her faults, but otherwise, it wasn't her face which drew people in. It was the music. If you could just close your eyes, you'd see the real Georgia. She always believed that.

The first set went great. She and Nambi played some of their regulars, a cover of 'Superstitious' that crowds raved about, with a lot of added twists to make it their own. Like Manu said, the best was when their music played off each other and with each other, bouncing around like atoms that wouldn't settle. The energy they created reached out into the crowd, and they were rewarded with cheers and whistles. Then there was a composition of Nambi's, where she stepped back and just gave him space for his solo. People loved it, more than just the occasional looking up from their dinners. She actually saw one guy drop his mouth open, fork suspended, as he watched Nambi do his thing. It was like Nambi was in another world of his own creation, where the rhythm just took hold and ran away with him.

That made Georgia so happy – for Nambi, for herself as his partner, and for Kai, whose experimental night was turning out to be a big success. Kai was back in the corner with the mixing board. He looked up and caught her eye, giving a thumbs up and a wide smile.

They took a break, and she went to the toilets to splash some water on her face. She was wired from the Red Bull and vodka. She knew she shouldn't have accepted a second one, but what the hell. Her energy always rose during the second set, building to a crescendo and then crashing right after the final note. Every time, it was the same. But it was no problem, as long as she hung on long enough.

Georgia went into a stall. Some women were talking by the basins, too loudly. They can't have known she was there because one said to the other, 'The music is great. The drummer is so hot. But the girl, have you ever seen anyone so ugly on stage?'

Georgia's face flashed hot as she sat, knickers down, frozen. Could she defend herself? Not a chance.

'She's not so bad. Really good on the sax, don't you think?'

'Maybe, but you know, jazz really isn't my thing. And she should be behind the curtain, not front and centre. Get someone else to front the band, someone more pleasing on the eye.'

'That's so rude! It's not as if you can play anything.'

'At least I know my place. The problem with girls like that is no one has put them in their place yet.'

Georgia had to get out of there. Fuck those women, the hypocrites coming to a jazz night and not caring at all about the music. She flushed the toilet and stood up. Smoothed down her t-shirt and pulled back on her favourite jeans, the ones that usually gave her courage.

When she came out to the basins to wash her hands, the women were gone.

She looked at her face in the mirror. It was ugly, she knew that. No one had ever said otherwise. Red hair that could never be fully tamed. Eyes a bit too far apart and too big for her face. Tiny mouth that no lipstick could fix. Had to have a bunch of teeth pulled to make room for the remaining ones. That's why she wasn't a singer, didn't have the mouth for it. And she knew that playing the sax does things to your neck muscles, your cheeks. Subtle changes, but they were the price you pay for making the beautiful sounds. If people didn't realise that, then fuck them.

She came back for the second set and asked a waitress for another Red Bull and vodka.

'You sure?' Nambi gave her a questioning look, but she pretended not to see.

When the drink came, she put it down on the floor next to her amp. She needed the courage to go on. She noticed two women sitting at a small table to the side, near the front. One had a high black ponytail and pouty lips. The other was blonde with hair blown so straight it could have been a wig. There was something about them. Georgia just knew they were the ladies from the loo. Unmistakable. When the blonde put her lacquered fingernails to her lips to whistle as Kai announced Nambi for the second set, it was clear.

Georgia tried to put them out of her mind. It didn't matter what she looked like. It never mattered. Her currency was the music, the energy, the improvising with Nambi that happened every time. It had never gone wrong before, wouldn't start now. She and the sax were the voice, Nambi and his drums were the rhythm. Nothing could disrupt that.

Everything was okay. Not the best, but okay. They got through a few songs and then each had a solo. Nambi was killing it. She stood back and watched his efforts, the subtle smile on his face as he closed his eyes in concentration and just let the music lead. He was in his element. He was jazz, in all the ways Georgia had been taught.

Then it was time for her last solo of the evening and she felt a flutter of doubt, something she hadn't experienced in a long time. Indecision about where to go with the music never affected her before, but as she let it meander and took a pause, she heard one voice over all the other diners.

'...see what I mean? She'd be better off hiding that face behind the curtain.'

Georgia's breath failed. She couldn't believe that fate would carry *those* particular words to her ears, above any other whispers of approval or encouragement. She let the sax die to nothing as she looked up at the two women. The blonde was looking at her phone, but the black-haired one had her eyes on Georgia with what could only be described as spite.

She had wanted Georgia to hear. To stab her with those words. No question about it.

Nambi continued playing, looking up nervously and whispered, 'George?'

But Georgia couldn't do anything other than stare at the woman. She dropped her hands to her hips and let the sax hang from its strap.

Nambi kept playing in a holding pattern; some diners looked up with puzzled expressions.

A red rage rose to block the music, Georgia's limbs and arms under its control. She walked in front of their table, holding the black-haired woman's stare.

Nambi stopped. The whole place stopped. It seemed as though no one moved or breathed.

'What did you say?' asked Georgia.

The blonde looked up from her phone and then put her hand on her friend's arm. 'Shit,' she said quietly. 'She heard you.'

Ponytail woman tried to hide it. 'I didn't say anything.' She shook off her friend's grasp.

'What did you just say about me?' Georgia's volume rose. She would not be deflected.

'Look, this is totally uncalled for,' Ponytail looked left and right for support.

'You should be ashamed of yourself!' Georgia struggled to find the words. Her heart was beating too fast, her breathing too shallow. 'Saying things about a performer's looks. When everyone knows music... music doesn't care about how you look!'

'Look, honey,' Blondie tried to diffuse the situation. 'She didn't mean anything.'

'Yes, she did! I heard her in the toilets! She didn't care who else heard either!' Georgia was out of control now, she knew it but couldn't help it. Her arms flailed around, trying to make an impact.

She stepped forward, not to do anything to the women, but to assert herself, make herself taller. To be stronger, be the bigger woman.

But a Red Bull can on the floor tripped her up, and she tumbled forward.

Ponytail shrieked and shielded herself as Georgia tipped to the side. Her sax, still on its strap, slammed against the bistro table-top, shattering the glass in a round pattern as if a bullet had hit.

'Wait, Georgia, wait!' Kai came running. 'Are you hurt?'

Georgia put her hand down and felt a sharp pain as a glass edge sliced her palm.

The red rage dissolved. She knew she had been totally unprofessional. She'd let a real-life troll with fancy makeup get to her, and it had ruined the set. Ruined her partnership – what if Nambi wouldn't play with her again? Probably Kai would drop them like a ton of bricks.

Georgia did not resist as Kai lifted her to her feet. She cradled her bleeding hand in the rolled-up hem of her shirt.

'You're hurt!' Nambi was at her side, concern all over his face.

It was only then they saw, all three at once, that the bell of her sax was damaged, probably beyond repair. Its round lip was smashed and bent inwards, as if someone had been determined to choke off the music. Georgia moved to try to un-bend it, but yelped in pain.

'We need to get you to A&E,' Kai said. She had no words left, no objection. 'Sorry' wouldn't fix it. It didn't matter that she had been right, and that woman embodied the opposite of everything that jazz stood for. Everything Georgia had lost.

She couldn't move. Her bandaged hand lay flat above the covers, throbbing and heavy. The rest of her body was like cement, never going to shift again. She had broken her sax beyond repair. It had been a gift from Manu; well, not totally free but a friend of his who was retiring had wanted to sell it on to an aspiring musician at a good price. He wanted the instrument to play on, he said, and she couldn't believe her luck back then.

But luck can run out, especially when your mentor leaves town. And if you happen to be the ugliest girl who ever tried to make it in South London's jazz scene.

She would never be able to afford a new sax. They cost thousands and thousands of pounds, and she didn't earn anything close to what she'd need. And who would pay her to perform now? She knew it would be all over social media already. She wasn't aware of much after she hurt her hand, but she did notice that people were filming her, making fun of her. Nambi told them to stop but it didn't matter. She was finished.

The ceiling crack began to blur as her eyes stung with bitterness. A tear formed and she willed it to make up its mind, either go down her cheek or evaporate, but don't just stay there, messing with her vision.

Her phone kept pinging with notifications. She was probably being trashed on Instagram, YouTube and TikTok all at the same time. She didn't move, just noticed the street noise from the road below and the sound of her housemates slamming the bathroom door.

Her phone rang, and she let it go to voicemail. But it rang again and eventually she had to pick up.

There were loads of texts from Nambi, and from Kai too. All checking she was okay, asking about her hand. Lots of notifications from Instagram where she'd been tagged, she didn't want to see those.

Nambi rang again, while she was holding it in her good hand, and she felt like she couldn't reject him.

He started talking as soon as she picked up. 'George, how's the hand? Are you okay? Why haven't you answered my texts?'

She opened her mouth to reply but couldn't think of how to sum it all up. 'It's over Nambi. My sax is finished.'

'George, listen, have you seen what's happening on TikTok?'

'People had their phones out, probably it's the worst. I can't face it.'

'No, it's not like that. Someone did record the confrontation, to be honest. And that girl, she was a proper bitch. She tried to post it, trolling you.'

'Why are you telling me this?'

'Because listen: so many people came out and trolled her back. Someone who had recorded part of the set earlier and said it was some of the best sax they'd ever seen. Someone else confirmed that the girl is a real arsehole. Has no real friends. Just likes to post selfies on social media with her mouth in a pout as if she's a fashion model. But Tik Tok is turning on her. Look at this, I'll send it to you.'

A message pinged through, with a link.

'Watch it then call me right back.'

Georgia clicked on the link and saw the face of Ponytail woman. She had 15k followers and seemed to only post photos of herself. Go figure. Her latest one with the #outtacontrol hashtag has her speaking to camera, with a fake distraught look, saying, 'This girl, Georgia, she just stopped the whole set. Stopped the whole set and walked up to me and attacked me. Smashed the glass and everything. I thought I was gonna die!'

That was *so* not true, but who would the world believe? An influencer with thousands of followers, or an ugly jazz player who can no longer play? Ponytail troll had 1.5k likes, but what was interesting was how the number was going down as you watched. And the comments were going up. Many of them were saying negative stuff about Ponytail woman.

Georgia sat up, and clicked on the trend #outtacontrol and found a huge number of Tiktokkers suddenly taking interest. One posted a video of her and Nambi earlier in the set, when she was really going for it in her solo. No extra comments, just a thumbs up and the fire emoji and the hashtags #jazzonfire #straightouttapeckham and #uglygirlsunite

Ugly girls? Georgia laughed at that, despite herself. Did someone else hear the troll talking about her? She clicked on some other links, following #jazzonfire and seeing more clips of her playing, also of others in the music scene that she knew and looked up to: Charlie Jamera, Lee Frank, and others. She clicked on #uglygirlsunite and up popped a face of a red-haired girl with crazy curls that defied gravity. She talked about how she couldn't stand the stereotypes against red-heads and how they needed to reclaim their beauty.

Georgia didn't know about reclaiming or any of that. She just wanted to play sax again. After following a few more links she cheered up slightly, but was still paralysed about what to do next. She rang Nambi back.

'Look, Georgia, I don't know what happened in the ladies yesterday, but I just hope you're okay. A lot of people heard her bitching about you, and they're standing up for you.. You know why? Because you're the best sax player I've ever played with, and...' he hesitated, before blurting out: 'You're my best friend. I can't play without you. I need you to get better. No one cares what you look like. Or, actually, I do, but you're not ugly! I don't care what one shitty troll says.'

Georgia could hear him breathing, as if worried he'd said too much.

'I think my hand will be okay,' she said. 'They glued it back together and all. I haven't peered beneath the bandages yet though. But –'

'But?'

'But my sax, Nambi. It's totally messed up. I'm nothing without my sax. And there's no way I can afford another.'

'Look, Georgia, I get it. You haven't had the chance to see the news. Go on Insta and look at the reels. See what Kai has done for you, for us. He says we are one of his best acts, can't let young talent go to waste.'

She switched over to Instagram and saw so many notifications. People had tagged the performance yesterday, but also earlier shows. #straightouttapeckham was trending, as well as #uglygirlsunite and #gingerjazz . She wasn't sure where this was going. She clicked on Kai's profile, where she was tagged.

He did a piece speaking straight to camera. Said Georgia and Nambi were one of the most promising acts he had seen this year, and their set yesterday was probably the best yet.

'But it's such a shame that an accident at the end put Georgia in hospital and broke her instrument. Without her instrument, she can't play. And if she can't play, then these two can't make their beautiful music, and that would be such a damn shame for the whole London jazz scene. Because they have something really special. Together they have the alchemy that almost no one has at that age. We have to raise the money to get Georgia a new sax and put her right back up there on stage again.'

He'd started a crowdfunder last night, must have been when he got home after paying for the taxi to A&E. The goal was £2000, more than enough for a sax from Headwind Music in Bristol, the best shop in the country for second-hand equipment. He had already raised £800 and it hadn't even been 24 hours. Where was the money coming from?

She clicked through to the crowdfunder page, and there was a wide range of small donations. £5 here, £7.50 there. Some people left their names, she wasn't sure if she recognised them: Katie J, Sam F. Some left messages for Kai, others for her and Nambi. Some just left the hashtags. Some were anonymous. Nambi had given £20, he didn't have to do that.

She rang him. 'I'm blown away,' she said. 'How did Kai do all of that while I was sleeping?'

'Well, it is 2 pm,' he teased her. 'I guess all that Red Bull wears off eventually.'

'I'm sorry I ruined our set,' she said. 'I shouldn't have let what she said get to me.'

'It's okay, you're only human. I guess I should've known you couldn't be perfect all the time.'

'Perfect? Hardly. With my hair and fashion sense? I'm nowhere near perfect.'

'Don't you see, your music surrounds you. It is you. When you play, that's all people see. But I see it all; I get the close-up, backstage pass-view. And if I still think you're amazing, well,' his voice softened, 'that should be worth something.'

'Aww, stop. You're making me blush.'

'Enough of that. Can we meet for brunch? My treat.'

'Hang on. I haven't even got up yet. I need to shower, but I'm not sure what I can do with this bandage.'

'You'll think of something. A plastic bag over it, for a few days. We'll get you back playing before you know it.' Nambi hung up.

She started to stand up, then reconsidered and went back onto the crowdfunder site. More names had been added, including one for £50 that said just 'M.L.'

Her heart sped up, knowing only one person with those initials. How had Manu seen the crowdfunder? He wasn't on social media, right? She really wanted to talk to him, to play with him again. But he'd be disappointed that she'd broken the sax he'd given her, beyond repair. That's not what a legacy was. Legacy was looking after things, for the next generation of jazz.

Or maybe legacy was different from that. Maybe legacy was more basic and elemental. About the seeds of something. The inspiration of something. A legacy could be a memory. It could be music. A story that sets a young person off on a pursuit in their own way.

Georgia stood up and stretched, looking at her reflection in the mirror. You, she told herself, you are a jazz musician. You're not an influencer or a TikTok star or a fashion icon. Some may find you ugly, others don't mind or see past that. Or just have a different opinion. You were Manu's protégé. You are Nambi's best friend. And you are going to be #jazzonfire, again, as soon as you can sort out the time to take the coach to Bristol.

THE PROMISED LAND

STEVYN COLGAN

I awoke and I knew that I was no longer on Earth.

I could feel the sun upon my back and the warm sand between my fingers and, though every part of me ached and my heart thundered in my chest, I forced my head up to look around me.

What a sight greeted my eyes!

From horizon to horizon there was nothing but sand. But this was not the dull, dun-coloured sand of Earth; it was a scintillating carpet of colour, a dazzling miasma of reds and golds, greens and deep blues. It was as if a million precious gems had been crushed to dust in order to cover the land. Gold nuggets the size of peas lay scattered about. The elements we value so highly on our world were just so much litter here. I grabbed a handful and let what felt like immeasurable wealth trickle through my fingers. I ventured a laugh but a sudden nausea overcame me and I was violently sick. My head began to spin and my vision blurred. Eventually, the convulsions subsided and I was again able to force my head up to examine my new surroundings. Pinkish clouds drifted lazily across a lemon yellow sky. There were no trees, no birds, no sounds at all. Where was I? Was it Mars perhaps? Or Venus? Perhaps some moon of Jupiter or Saturn? I didn't know.

All I did know was how I had arrived here.

My name is Adam Fox and there are those who will say that I am a wicked man. Perhaps I am? I don't dispute it. But I firmly believe that many people would do as I did, had they found themselves in the same dire predicament.

At first, there were few outward signs; an occasional dizzy spell, the odd nosebleed. But when I collapsed at the theatre, I knew that something was terribly wrong. At the time, I assumed it to be due to my overworking and lack of sleep. Ah, such wishful thinking! Confirmation of my worst fears arrived when I was examined by Dr Laxby of Harley Street. I had contracted a form of cancer and I was given less than a year to live.

Desperation will do strange things to even the best of men.

I sought solace in religion but the church could offer me nothing but a promise of eternal life in the hereafter. That, of course, is what we all hope for but I wanted a full span of earthly life before I got my wings. I was young, rich and successful. I wanted to love and be loved, to explore new lands, to experience new thrills, to discover new tastes and desires. I couldn't give all of that up just for some ephemeral dream of what might be. Even the looming threat of war did not diminish my lust for life. So I began to look elsewhere. Call me foolish; call me a madman, but accept that I was an impetuous thirty-year old man; a drowning man, despairingly clutching at straws.

I sought out people who purported to hold mystic powers and arcane knowledge. I scoured libraries and dusty book shops in search of ancient tomes of magick. And, eventually my researches led me to a book, supposedly bound in human skin, that was alleged to contain a spell that could transport my soul into another body. I used my life's savings to acquire the book. I was desperate. My condition had become so much worse.

On the night of January 12th 1913, I sat naked on the floor of my drawing room and waited for midnight. I had torn up the carpet in order to draw an arcane pentagram upon the parquet. The furniture had been taken away by the Rag and Bone that evening. One way or another, I'd not need them for much longer. The snow was falling heavily and the wind howled in the chimneys as a perfect backdrop to this, my act of heresy.

Being so close to death, they say, clears the mind. Certainly, I was lucid and, if not quite sane, I felt no loss of mental acuity. I had even made provisions for the possibility of failure. A bottle of barbiturate and a syringe lay beside me. The pain had become much worse of late. If this did not work, I would be in pain no longer.

The clock chimed twelve and I painfully shuffled into the centre of the pentangle. A sudden chill wind caught me unawares and I shivered. Then, a great gust seemed to rise up from nowhere and reddened the ashes in the hearth. I began to chant.

A feeling of utmost calm overcame me. I surrendered to its warm and comforting embrace and let it envelop my frail, failing body. A fierce pressure pushed at my temples and unseen hands seemed to pull me in all directions at once. I screamed for them to stop. Then all was dark. Was this death come to claim me, I wondered?

And then, after what might have been seconds or years, I had awoken here, in this strange place, and I knew that the spell had succeeded. My soul had been drawn from my failing body and deposited... where? And into what vessel? I realised that this was not my body. This was a strong, powerful body. I could see a torso clothed in a mat of dark hair and a defined, well-developed musculature. My hands were large and powerful.

And I was alive! Alive!

I was wishing for the throbbing of my head to pass, when I became aware that I was no longer alone.

I looked up and was astonished to see that it was a woman. Her skin was white – almost blue – like fine porcelain. Her face was framed with jet black hair that cascaded over her shoulders. She was tall and willowy in her frail elegance, and she was very beautiful. At her side stood a fantastic beast that I can scarce describe, save to say that its head was equipped with a tooth-lined jaw so capacious that it could swallow a man whole. I suddenly remembered a serialised story I'd read in *All-Story Magazine*, about a Confederate soldier who was mysteriously transported to an alien world where he met a beautiful princess. I tried to remember whether the tale had ended happily.

The girl approached, perhaps sensing that I posed her no threat, and looked at me with curiosity writ large upon her face.

'Garathrey set darhaija?'

It sounded like a question, but I had no answer. The hammering in my temples was so loud as to drown all other sound. I clutched at my chest and tried to rise to my feet but I hadn't the strength and I collapsed to the sand. I forced my head up one last time.

I had travelled perhaps many millions of miles (or years maybe?) to a world that no Man born of Earth had ever seen. A world of strange beauty and wonder. A world where the precious stones of Earth were as pebbles. A world where at least one woman was more beautiful that any terrestrial maiden I had ever seen. A world that offered me a chance to be a man again, to do great deeds and reap vast rewards.

A world, in short, that offered me everything that the Earth could not. Everything, that is, except an adequate oxygen atmos...

(With humble apologies to Edgar Rice Burroughs, A Merritt, E E Doc Smith, Robert E Howard, Charles R Tanner and all of the other great pulp science fiction authors of the early 20th century.)

EVERYTHING IS MADE OF SOIL

ZENA BARRIE

I used to think, that one day I would be a pretty significant person. I never knew quite how, my only talent that could potentially set me apart from everyone else is the ability to make my ears make a popping sound and to have very bendy arms. This was never going to get me very far in life. Some people are maths geniuses or have music in their fingertips. I just have bendy arms, I've never been able to make a living from it and I suspect I never will.

It's fine, I've accepted my fate and am trying to make the best of it, I am not one of the Stephen Hawkings or George Michaels of this world, but I do have a party trick I can do on demand. Did they? (Yes, I know I know, singing and doing maths, fair enough).

I have accepted my fate as one of life's not-significant-people, and it feels ok. I now know that even the best of us just trend on twitter for a few hours or make the news if we've done something really special, and then what?

We don't get to hear of our death on the news or the local paper; we don't get to hear the speeches. If we live long enough, no-one will be alive that cares or remembers us. We will be desperate to die to get away from all the bloody people talking to us in a loud baby voice. As our skin gets thinner and starts to hang from our body, when no one wants to touch us anymore, we are devalued to just being some old person who has the audacity to still be alive; so many parts of us will already be gone.

Even now, in middle age, friends have died, and each of them took a piece of me with them, they didn't mean to, they just did.

They are no longer here to confirm or deny our shared history. If I don't tell anyone about it, did it ever happen? If I forget things and there is no one around to remind me of it, it's gone for good. If I change the story, no one can prove it. When their life flashed before them in their final moments, was I in the slide show? Did I make the cut? Popping my ears and bending my arms at school? Some memory they had about me has gone into the grave with them. That memory became liquid. Then soil. Indistinguishable now from anything else but made from memories. Sorry to make it about me, but I am the one thinking about this. I'm having an existential crisis here, can't you tell?

Look at the trees in graveyards. Fertilised by the bodies underneath them. Are their trunks filled with the DNA of the dead? Does every leaf know something you don't? Something they cannot repeat. Do they know anything about me? Have they seen me naked? They might have. They might know me better than anyone else. Thank goodness trees can only communicate with other trees. How far have they spread their gossip? Has the news of my bendy arms made its way to the Amazon rain forest through a complicated system of roots?

Once we are dead, any stories that are told about us won't be for our ears. If someone secretly loved us, loathed us, or even worse, were indifferent to us, we will never know... Ask them now!

Do you secretly love me?

Oh.

Do you loathe me?

Do you feel indifferent towards me?

Ah, I see.

Thank you for that information.

Or does that just make things awkward?

A cemetery opens early and holds cremation after cremation after cremation all day long. Friends and family walk in through the front and leave weeping through the back.

Every family walks in with a CD of the greatest hits of Frank Sinatra. "Could you play 'That's Life' on the way in and 'I Did it My Way' on the way out please?"

And did you? Did you do it *your* way? Was it *very* different? Was it? How different could it possibly be? You probably still slept and got up, did your morning ablutions and then got on with your day, earned some money to pay for food and then went to bed later on? Am I right? Perhaps I am psychic, maybe I have a special skill after all?

What song will get chosen for me? I hope there is an interpretive dance to go with it. I'd like everyone to wear flesh coloured body suits and neutral masks. Push back the pews and really make the space their own. Have some mushrooms and get catatonic whilst my body burns… That's something I wouldn't mind watching. Damnit.

We are yellow-spined dog-eared books on a shelf. We are fading photographs in a box if we ever even got printed, and if no one wrote a name on the back of those photos, we are a nameless person from the past, look at our funny hair! You may have been carefully stuck into a photograph album but someone will chuck you away eventually when they have absolutely no idea who you were.

We are an anecdote that changes every time until it's not told anymore.

We are a ghost on the internet. Google us and we are still there. We've just been inactive for a very long time. We'll be stored on some outdated computer system in a basement somewhere and when that technology fails, as it is as fallible as us, it will take our last ghostly internet imprints with it.

Break us down to our elements and we are, at most; a bucket of blood, an unsightly mound of streaky bacon. A pile of bones. Some gristle.

We are all skeletons covered in tracksuits that buy birdfeeders, so we can watch the birds, watch the beautiful birds from our kitchen window whilst we cook the birds, eat the birds and scrape the remains of the birds into the bin.

We are so deluded we wear clothes with skeletons painted on them. Entirely forgetting about the skeleton that lies an inch behind a layer of meat that wouldn't even taste good.

We are blood, pints and pints of blood swashing around a skeleton, covered with a layer of lard and skin, half the time just lying unconscious on a mattress.

But oh, we think we're really something. Admit it. You're probably thinking 'well maybe *she's* nothing because all she can do is pop her ears but It's not like that for me, I can do 50 squats and am excellent at paint ball'.

No one cares.

We get on planes and go to other countries and park our walking butchers' shop on the beaches and we lightly cook ourselves as our hugely anticipated annual recreation. Let's all sit in a sand pit with strangers and change colour. Then go back to work and say "Oooh yes, I had a lovely time changing colour, I saved all year so I could fly off and sit in a sand pit and change colour, are you going away soon? Which sand pit are you going to? Ooh lovely, you'll really change colour when you go there, my mate went there and you wouldn't believe how much she changed colour and she said the sand pit was lovely."

We are all skeletons wearing sequins to disguise the blood, and meat and bones.

We spend our lives collecting things that are all made of... soil.... And that one day... will be soil again. Just like we will. Just like parts of us already are. We're already half way there.

We live in the vain hope of leaving something behind. Some memory of us. That we were. Here. Against all the odds and all the evidence.

Even though, 2000 years ago we remember Jesus and Judas. The good man and the bad man. Then we don't remember anyone else until Shakespeare. And then if you're honest who do you remember? Samuel Pepys? The man who wrote a diary whilst his street burnt down?

Napoleon? Some French dude with one arm? Or was that Nelson? One of them has a column, one of them has one eye, I know that much.

We will not be remembered, that is the truth of it. And everything we own will turn back into soil via the charity shop.

We are blood and meat and bones in blue jeans. And we judge each other on the type of jeans we wear to cover up all of the meat we're trying to hide underneath.

We are hair and teeth and nails and we wear fake hair, fake teeth, fake nails trying to disguise our decay. Our journey back to the ground. No one wants to looks like the aged animal they are.

We are rejection. The first pieces set out their stall and build a base camp. By the time we are forty the walls are high, with guards and look outs and warning signals, a sentry sits there with buckets of burning oil to fling when necessary. They hit the air and turn into self-deprecating jokes as they land. We have to use the jokes, burning oil is not socially acceptable, even if you smile whilst you pour it.

That collection you have? The one you've spent 30 years on? Porcelain pigs from all over the world? Your children hate them. They will give them away with delight. They will get broken and separated in the charity shop. A child will walk in and buy part of your collection with their 50 pence pocket money. The pig will go in their toy box. It will get broken. The mother will be glad it's broken, it is not to her taste and she will gleefully throw the sharp pieces into the bin. One less bit of tat to look at. I know this to be true, I bought one fancy-spoon from someone's beloved fancy-spoon collection and then put it in the dishwasher. It's a utilitarian spoon now. The owner would turn in their grave if they weren't already liquid. They'd shout "Don't separate my fancy-spoon collection, that's my life's work you motherfucker!" Perhaps the trees are silently screaming this whenever I walk past them. I hope not, I hope they don't hold grudges in their branches. They should learn to get over it.

We are humiliation, we are a silo of every humiliation that ever took place in our lives. We store it for a lifetime we keep the lid on tight because if we lose the lid, or anything spills out we feel all of it and no one wants it, no one wants to be around it. No one wants to feel *that*. We can't even watch people on the television being humiliated, or be about to be humiliated. We have to watch from behind a pillow. At least I do, has it ended yet? We don't want to see it in case we feel it with them. We store it for a lifetime, an unwelcome visitor we can't get rid of.

We date, and we talk and laugh and pretend we're interested in a thousand different things. He looks nice, he likes red wine (but not too much red wine), reading books (but nothing you'd buy in a supermarket), making nice meals from the River Cottage cook book and going for long walks. He's disguised all of his meat underneath a nice jumper. He's no stranger to a William Morris pattern and he doesn't look violent, sounds like a keeper!

But do we know what we actually care about? Really? I like politics, but mostly for the tittle tattle. Is it the drama that I like? Is it politicians being humiliated? Am I *that* person? Oh come on, we are ALL that person? Given the chance would I be prisoner turned lunatic guard? I'm probably not as nice as I think I am. Be warned.

We are all those bits of Tupperware from takeaways when you couldn't be bothered to cook.... Oh no... you won't cook because this pile of blood and meat and bones wants to be waited on. This is a lazy pile of meat. And what was that you say? You want to order what? Oh, just some other meat to stuff in your body made of meat. In fact, three different kinds of meat. So you sit there pushing ducks and chickens and cows down your human meaty throat. And then you fall asleep because when human meat needs to digest cows and pigs and ducks, it takes time. And we keep cats and dogs as pets and feed them on chickens and cows and fish all mushed up together and pressed into pretty shapes.

We are really really weird.

And when we see people on holiday. Lying on the beach, getting pink in the sun and showing off their rolls of meat that had hitherto been disguised, we hold our noses. Do we want to be reminded of all of that... skin... that flesh... that meat. Is that what we look like? Is that what we are? Am I really just a barrel of blood? I feel like I am more... I think therefore I... have a brain... a fleshy mushy brain. We've been tricked into thinking we are more. Evolution has really fucked us up. Those chimps at Chester Zoo look happy, why can't we just do what they do? I wouldn't mind the cage so long as it was big enough and electric blankets could be made available... and good internet connection of course, oh and I suppose I'd like my thumbs to be opposable if possible, so I can still play thumb wars.

We walk around shedding cells, so many there is a constant storm taking place around us. The Great Shedding. We leave pieces of us behind on everything we touch. We spend a lifetime filling our brains, striving to be better, we try to fill ourselves up with all the best stuff, read the best books, eat the good food, speak to the right people, we pride ourselves on having good brains that make fast connections.

It takes three minutes to empty out a lifetime of knowledge. For it to turn to mush. To liquid. To water. To something we wouldn't eat. Those connections we were so proud of? All that time at university... all of that trying and failing and succeeding and failing again. Of love and loss and getting over that pain and grief and tears and expansion... of getting fit and getting fat and getting fit again. Of falling out and falling in and glowing up and growing out and growing down.

It's all gone.

Any secrets you held you finally release. They are liquid now. If someone found one, they wouldn't be able to decipher it.

We are made of blood and meat and bones, all of us, but we pride ourselves on our differences.

There are no differences.

We are all just trying.

We are all just pretending.

Passing the time until we are soil again

And who knows what we'll come back as? Maybe if we're lucky we'll be a tree next time, much less frantic, more longevity, we would get better with age, we would be around to see what happens and we wouldn't go grey. Then someone will come along and chop us down and make us into a bed. And have sex on us and sleep on us not knowing that the bed they lie on is full of human remains that once held secrets and told lies and sung in the car and ate meat and lived a life and died a death.

And that bed will fall apart and it will go to the tip and a seagull will land on us and we will not know and no one will care.

You give your baby toasted soldiers made with bread made from wheat grown on ancient battlefields and wonder why he cries at night.

Someone visits you and says, "your baby has wise eyes." In fact, you all agree he has wise eyes. "That one's been here before," someone else says. And you all nod in agreement. And even though you are a rational person, you think yes, my baby has lived many times before and holds an unimaginable store of wisdom, never mind that he screams all night, he is the oracle.

And of course he has been here before, and you have, and I have, bits of us have been here since the beginning of time. You've probably been an iceberg and passed through the body of Christ in the form of a fish.... And then your wise oracle baby needs his nappy changing. Because for now, he is piss and shit and meat and blood and bones and so are you and so am I and so are we all.

But can I ask one thing of you? If you meet me, ask me to pop my ears for you, ask me to bend my arms? Let me have my moment in the sunshine. Be amazed at the popping sound. Be astounded at how far up my back my arms will go. Let me impress you, let me feel what it's like to be Beyonce for just one little moment, probably in some Manchester pub garden. Not that Beyonce would pop her ears and show off her bendy arms in a pub garden on request, but I will!

Then when I am on my death bed (let's hope it's a bed, I want to die in comfort) and I close my eyes and know my brief time of being alive on this planet is over, I will have a little greatest hits of my life video playing in my head. Frank Sinatra will sing and I will see black and white images of myself. Laughing and waggling my fingers whilst people stand around with their pints laughing too.

ARIEL

VIRGINIA MOFFATT

I f only she could be brave, thinks Juliet. If she were even a tiny bit brave, she would be at home watching Netflix leaving Roman to the adoring fans gathered for the launch of his game. Instead, she is standing beside him in the wings, watching the preview video on the large screen at the back of the stage, as a deep voice intones:

> *In the year 2050...*
> *...billionaires cower in bunkers...*
> *...as the flames they lit engulf the planet...*
> *...on the burning surface, terrified citizens cry out in fear...*
> *Will anyone answer their call?*

A young woman appears on the screen. She has a round face, big blue eyes, red pouty lips and long blond hair tied in a high ponytail. She is dressed in a tight one-piece jump suit that accentuates her large breasts and tiny waist. She is Juliet, but without all her imperfections.

> *From the volcanoes of Iceland to the rainforests of Brazil...*
> *.... the streets of San Francisco to the Serengeti Plain...*
> *there is only one person brave enough...*
> *...one person tough enough...*
> *... one woman who can save the planet...*

Ariel: Earth Defender

As the narrator speaks, Ariel swings over molten lava, fights arsonists in the forest, hoses down a blazing building, with speed and grace, the action hero Juliet could never be.

From the makers of Earth, and Air, comes,
ELEMENTAL PART 3: World on Fire
Available 1ˢᵗ November 2024

As the lights come up, Hugo Bracewell, owner of Activist-A Games walks onto the stage from the opposite wing. 'Welcome to the launch party of Elemental: World on Fire', he says. 'We're delighted to have you with us today. It looks incredible, doesn't it? And I can promise you it's *even* better than its predecessors. But before you get a chance to try it for yourselves, I know you want to hear from the creative duo at the heart of Elemental...

Roman Warner, game designer, philanthropist and activist extraordinaire...

and his beautiful muse, model and life partner, Juliet Emory!'

Roman grabs her hand and they stride forward to meet their audience, who whoop with delight at the sight of their favourite celebrity couple. Roman is wearing a light blue jacket, over a blue, floral, open-necked shirt, and pale canvas trousers. Juliet is dressed in her Ariel costume, as buxom and slender as her avatar. During the shooting of the first Elemental (Grounded in the Earth) Roman had insisted she had breast implants, but he had them removed after one was ruptured in a sword fight. Nowadays, Ariel's body shape is achieved by use of a corset and push up bra. Juliet always has to look the part and judging by the applause, the effort is appreciated. The couple sit down as Hugo embarks on the Q&A.

As ever, Roman relishes this opportunity to talk about himself, how he develops his games, the wonder of their creative and romantic partnership, while Juliet sits in quiet terror. Even though she knows what she has to say, how to nod at the right time, smile in the right way so they present the perfect image to the world, her heart is racing the whole time they are on stage. It doesn't matter that if she falters, Roman is always there with a tight squeeze of the hand to ensure everything goes smoothly as always, she hates the limelight, made worse by the constant fear that she will end up saying the wrong thing.

'So, tell me, Roman, where do you get your ideas from?'

'Everywhere. Could be a news story, or watching Discovery Channel, a scientific article that excites me, or watching extreme sport,' he presses his large hand firmly on Juliet's, reminding her of her cue,

'And of course, his incredible imagination', she says, dutifully though she'd love to add, *with no little help from the strings of interns who pass through the team each year, none of whom are ever credited or dare to challenge for fear of Attack-A's infamous blacklist.* She doesn't dare, for more personal reasons. If she were as courageous as Ariel, she'd tell the truth, about Attack-A and Roman and the state of their relationship. But it's not in her nature. Which Roman well knows, and is why he can be confident she will smile sweetly beside him confirming, *yes, Roman did pick me off the streets* (poetic licence, she was sofa surfing*); yes, I do all my own stunts* (Roman insists); *yes, we take great care with safety and have an excellent track record* (Roman covers up the accidents, Juliet, the scars). On and on the interview goes. Same old questions, same old half-truths in reply. It's amazing anyone hasn't rumbled them yet, but that's Roman for you, master storyteller, always in control of the narrative.

At last, it is over and there is only the after party to be endured, fake laughs, banal chit chat and too much champagne. Thankfully, not for too long. Tomorrow, they are heading to Canada to begin filming Ariel's next adventure and even Roman recognizes an early night is required if they are to make the first flight. At 10pm, he grabs her hand, smiling and laughing as he leads her out to the limousine, giving her a kiss in front of the cameras before they get in. He drops her hand the minute they drive off.

'You did well tonight,' he says curtly, taking out his laptop and putting his headphones on. Once she would have been devastated by his lack of interest, but five years of living with Roman has destroyed any semblance of affection she once had for him. Now their relationship is simply part of the performance that goes with the job of being Ariel. For a long time, she's been resigned to that fact, believing him when he tells her she's no place else to go, that she couldn't survive a week without him, and putting up with his occasional fits of physical rage. But San Francisco changed all that. Roman was so focused on getting the perfect shot, he almost left it too late to get her out of the burning building. She was lucky to escape with second degree burns on her legs and weeks of breathlessness and skin irritation from smoke inhalation. She realized then, that if they carry on like this, one day, this job is going to kill her.

Back at the house, Roman disappears to the study, leaving Juliet to go to bed alone to consider the conundrum that has been on her mind since the fire. How is she going to leave him? She has no family, and since Roman cut her off from her social circle, no friends to run to. He controls her bank account, her passport, her access to the outside world. And he'll not let her go easily. The only thing she can use is her knowledge of the way he works – the harassment and serious injury cases, the NDAs for staff and bribes for local officials – but she needs evidence.

She knows it's there, in the files he has locked away on his computer, but she needs the passwords from his phone. She's fairly sure she can get them, having memorised the opening pattern, but both phone and laptop are never out of his sight during the day. And since she wears a body cam constantly to record her every move, forces her to wear a tracker, and the house has cameras in every room, there is no chance of trying while he is asleep. She will have to wait until they're in the cabin by the lake. Occasionally, when they are in remote places, he is less security conscious, perhaps he will be there. It's a ridiculously faint hope but it's all she's got; she falls asleep clinging to it.

Her hope is quashed the moment they arrive in the cabin. After an arduous journey – first class flight having long since lost its appeal – she immediately notices the lockable desk in the study and the cameras in every room. Unless she can disable the security, she's never going to get access. She hides her frustration with a smile to ensure Roman doesn't suspect a thing, wishing, not for the first time, that she really *was* Ariel. Ariel would know how to do it; she knows how to do everything. Unfortunately, tampering with electrical equipment is the one skill Roman hasn't insisted she learn. She will just have to wait till a better opportunity presents itself.

The cabin lies at the base of the mountain. It's on three levels with large glass windows facing in every direction. Behind them is the track they drove down, the driveway and tall pine trees packed closely together. In front of them, a long deep blue lake, surrounded by mountains covered in forest. Working on Elemental is so intense, that Juliet rarely gets a moment to consider her surroundings; she cannot ignore them here, this place is astonishing. She gasps with delight when she looks out at the view; even Roman seems impressed and for a moment she thinks they might be able to enjoy the sunset. But to her disappointment, he immediately turns back towards the table, 'Time for work'.

Over a heated-up frozen lasagna, they study the map of the lake, identifying which shipwreck they will investigate first. Most of the filming will take place when the crew arrive in two days, but Roman always likes to do one shoot which is just the two of them. He lightly dismisses Juliet's concerns that without back up they are placing themselves at risk. She knows better than to argue, but it confirms her conviction that one of these days,

Roman will be the death of her. She sleeps badly, full of dread for the day ahead and where his recklessness will lead.

But in the morning, when she wakes up to sunshine and bird song, the beauty of the lake calms her. The water is still and the air warm. Breakfasting with Roman on the deck watching a pair of eagles fly in the azure sky above them, she finds herself agreeing that conditions are perfect, they're going to have a great day. They pack the car and drive to Kootenay. At the beach, they change into their scuba gear, test oxygen tanks, bodycams and acoustic equipment and walk forward till they are deep enough to swim and then begin the descent.

Under the surface, the water is cold, but not too cold, and surprisingly clear, revealing a turquoise world of fish and weeds that is easy to navigate. For the first time in weeks Juliet feels calm and happy. This is so much better than Ariel's previous adventures, and she surprises herself by being as good as her instructor had said she was. She swims with a grace and strength she didn't know she possessed. For once, she feels she _is_ Ariel and appreciates Roman capturing her movements on camera. She wants to remember this.

It takes them fifteen minutes to reach the wreck. Their spare oxygen tanks will give them half an hour to explore, which is not much room for error, even in a lake as shallow as this. Even so, Juliet can't help slowing down to enjoy their surroundings, and to make the most of being in control of what they do. The upper decks have collapsed, leaving piles of bloated wood but the lower deck is still standing, surrounded by pipework, wooden posts covered in weed and mud. Roman directs her path through the wreckage as they weave in and out between the posts, recording the sight of the paddle wheel, a rusting pipe, the remains of a wall and window. It's fascinating; being Ariel feels worthwhile, if only for this.

They are nearly finished when it happens. Twice now Roman has directed Juliet through the centre of the wreck for a speedy action shot, but he has missed it both times. On the third time, he swerves to catch her but instead cannons into a copper pipe. The collision sends him reeling through the water where he bangs his head on the wall, tumbling down the side to the bottom of the lake. He doesn't move. Juliet's first response is a flash of joy. This is her opportunity. They have only twenty minutes of oxygen left, who could blame her if she left him and saved herself? Then she realises how stupid that would be. He could recover any second, and if he knows she tried to leave, he will make her suffer. Besides, the body cams are recording everything, putting her at risk of prosecution. Worst of all, despite everything he has done, she couldn't do that to him, she couldn't do that to anyone. She's Ariel, isn't she? The woman who saves people. Even her enemies.

She checks her watch, nineteen minutes. No time to waste. She dives to the bottom, and drags him to the base of the boat, trying to calm her breathing and not waste oxygen. Seventeen minutes. She puts her arms under his shoulders so she is sitting behind him, leans into the wall so she can sit him upright. He is heavy, really heavy, but she is not going to give up now. Thirteen minutes... She's cutting it fine, but she can do it.

She takes a deep breath, makes sure she is holding him tight, presses her flippers against the side of the wall to give them momentum and thrusts them upwards. She can still see her watch. Twelve minutes. She keeps pushing with her feet in a firm, steady rhythm. Pull... breathe... thrust. Where earlier she slid through the water with ease, now she feels like she is swimming through treacle. Ten minutes. Pull... breathe... thrust. Ahead of her she can see the sun above the water. Her arms are aching and the knowledge of how little oxygen they have left is making her lungs hurt. Eight minutes. Pull... breathe... thrust. The surface is getting closer. *Come on Ariel, you can do it.* Six minutes. The ripples on the surface are tantalisingly close. Four minutes. Pull... breathe... and splash, they burst through the water. She rolls onto her back still holding him, pulling their mouthpieces off, gasping for air. Roman is still unconscious, but she can feel a faint breath. That's a relief. She floats for a couple of minutes to recover and then strikes out for the shore.

When she makes the beach, she pulls out his phone from the plastic pouch on his waist and calls search and rescue. They're quick to respond, promising a boat as soon as possible. All Juliet has to do is keep Roman warm until then. He is too heavy to undress so she dries him as best he can, rolls him on his side into the recovery position and covers him in her coat and a blanket she grabs from the car. Then she takes his body cam off and dresses herself. Despite the warmth of the sun, his skin is icy and though he is breathing he is barely conscious. He looks diminished. Somehow, he is no longer Roman, just another human being who needs her help. She builds a small fire out of the sticks on the shore, grateful that at least he had the foresight to have brought matches.

To get his core temperature up she massages his hands and feet, over and over. It's weird, she has touched his body so many times, now it's as if she is touching a stranger. A stranger she must try and keep alive. That one thought is all that matters and soon she loses herself to the rhythm of the motion of her hands, the smell of smoke and the sound of his shallow breathing. She is so focused on the task, that when the boat finally turns up, she registers it only after someone calls out to her twice.

The rescue team are quick and efficient. They have him wrapped and on a stretcher within minutes. After checking Juliet is fit enough to drive herself, and commending her on a job well done, they give her the details of the hospital and depart. She watches the boat speed across the lake until they are out of sight. She sits back down enjoying the sensation of the warm earth beneath her, the gentle movement of the waves on the lake, the cool breeze on her face. Then, she opens Roman's phone. She smiles when she finds the passwords and bank details exactly where she'd hoped they'd be. It is at that moment she realizes in performing her last rescue, Ariel has saved them both.

With Roman in hospital, she has plenty of time to enact her plan. She will gather the evidence she needs, take her bank card and passport, leave the GPS tracker in the house and get away as soon as she can. She might even leak footage of the accident so that her heroic act is sealed in the public consciousness before he has a chance to hit back. She smiles. The water sparkles back tempting her in. She checks her watch. She has enough time. She puts on her swimming costume and dives into the cool clear waters. Surfacing, she floats gazing up at the sky, thinking of the life that is to come, a life she is finally brave enough to live. She savours it for as long as she can, before turning over and striking for the shore.

It's time to go, and she has work to do.

THE ELEMENTS OF STYLE

SAMUEL DODSON

There was a time when having style alone could really pay the bills. Those were the boom times. Those were the times when we could fall asleep counting the piles of tips left for us by adoring fans; by kids with no hope and students desperate to find their way in the world. By lonely housewives and househusbands, bored office jockeys who spent afternoons dreaming of blowing their brains out over their co-worker's new computer.

For these people, style seemed impossible – a dream. A word they knew but couldn't hope to understand. They were lost, and they came to find themselves by observing us – we the beautiful, we the existential, we the witty, slick and never-ageing future of the world; we, the stylish. We the cool. We who wore torn-up leather jackets, slouched around with toothpicks in our mouths, sniffed glue and huffed balloons and popped E pills like tic-tacs. We flicked the Vs, smoked cigarettes down to the filter, wore sunglasses long after dark, drank gin and juice and traded 'mans with one another while listening to Strummer blaring out of large speakers. We read Camus and Baudrillard and struck elaborate poses to show we didn't give a fuck about anything.

In short, we had all the elements of style. The chemical, sub-atomic basis at the route of all cool. And we knew, with these fundamental building blocks in place, the system would take care of the rest. Style was in fashion; and fashion was booming.

But it's difficult to really act like you don't give a fuck about anything when you have all this style but not enough to pay the bills. When the bills are increasing and your wages haven't moved in years. When Cassie calls to tell you Shaun is running low on his medicine. When the crowds start to dry up and what you hear on the news – when the news makes it to you – is just one long list of the catastrophes we're failing to deal with. And when was the last time anybody even left us a tip?

Since style is no longer enough to bring in the credits, I'm going where the credits are: in style leadership and management. If I can just perfect the no fucks giving and get back into the groove with all the rest of it, I could show off that grade A charisma and finally get that promotion.

Of course, it's also difficult to really act like you don't give a fuck about anything when I really give a fuck about this promotion.

'Hey man, why the long face?' Zoe says first thing this morning as she makes her way into our shared quarters and public viewing space. She reaches out her arms and curls and uncurls her fingers, twisting her shoulders around and moving her head from side to side as she stretches out the tension caused by whatever strange position she slept in last night. I've seen her sleep – I know she sleeps strangely, all twisted up like a Geiger sculpture. At first I thought it was stylish, or assumed it was somehow ironic.

'Hey dude,' I reply. And hate myself for it. *Nobody* says 'dude' anymore. I need to buck up my game.

Zoe gives me a look. The kind that says, 'you need to buck your game up'. Don't I know it. Next thing she does is bend over and pick up the remote control for our speakers. She presses a couple of buttons. I brace myself. She points the remote nonchalantly over her shoulder and turns the speakers on.

The distortion erupts throughout our shared quarters. Small pebbles near my feet begin to vibrate and move across the floor. I try to resist the urge to place my hands over my ears. This is the latest in a new form of 'anti music' that Zoe has uncovered. She is currently working her way through the back catalogue of a band called *Thus spoke the sea monkeys of Zarathustra.* As far as I can tell, the point of their music is to make the moments when their music isn't playing seem like divinity itself. But what do I know that Zoe doesn't? Zoe has all the elements of style – her performance ratings and customer feedback data are through the roof – so do I place my hands over my ears to block out the sound? I do not. Do I ask her to turn it off? I do not. I ask her to turn it up.

Of course, she doesn't hear me. She starts to sing.

She draws breath into her diaphragm, her chest expanding to the point that her torn-up leather jacket raises ever so slightly. And with full breath, she begins to yell nonsense ululations that are neither in rhythm nor key with the rest of the distorted track playing around us.

'Can you kindly shut your mouth and turn that nightmare off?' Eddie yells as he walks in from his own separate area. He is wearing a stained and fraying vest top and baggy blue, beat-up boxer shorts with gaping holes that reveal his testicles whenever he sits down.

Zoe ignores him. Although her ululations do begin to, well, ululate more intensely.

Back in the days, Eddie was a true expert in the social graces required in our roles – quick with a sneer, able to hold an intense, detailed conversation about Marxist dialectics while rolling a joint without watching his fingers. He could slide out across the dance floor when required and move as though his joints had just been oiled by the finest mechanic. He was slick and quick and wore his mirror shades at all times of day, whether eating breakfast, in the shower, or taking an afternoon shit. In short: he had style.

I can't remember the last time I saw Eddie in shades.

'Zoe, I swear to God if you do this one more time I'm going to walk right out of here and head down that hill. I am out of here. I swear. You watch.'

But Eddie won't be out of here. He knows it and Zoe knows it and I know it. Eventually, Eddie comes and sits beside me and helps me roll a cigarette. We try to bop our heads along to the anti-music and hope that today might be the day that someone comes along to our enclosure.

They don't.

***

In the old days, back when Eddie was an Icon and before I needed a promotion, we'd mix and socialise with the others onsite. We'd go down to the Existentialist's café and drink apricot cocktails with JP and Simone. Or we'd have a BBQ at the Graceland enclosure and discover the joys of putting peanut butter on all our food. At night we'd join the speakeasy guys for their moonshine while listening to the best records. I remember Al was dating Ella at the time – she had all these dogs she'd rescued or just picked up along the way. And while we'd be talking and the smoke would be pooling in the arched ceiling above the bar, Al would stand up, take Ella by the hand and lead her out to this little dancefloor. And the sax would be growling over the beat of the drums and the keys would be working their way over our skin as we watched Ella rest her head on his shoulder and they'd drift together, feet moving in perfect sync, heart to heart.

Now though, with the big decline in fans – adoring or otherwise – everyone at Graceland has been sent to Administration, the Existentialist's café can't afford apricots, and the Speakeasies are all boarded up. We're not sure where Ella's gone, but most of her dogs have gone wild. You see them at the bins sometimes, tearing at rotting things.

***

Ours is somewhat of a stressful workplace. If your style rating drops too far, you're a goner.

Of course, this is all run by the algorithm. Punters hit their feedback buttons after scrutinising you in your enclosure – as is their right, of course, they've paid their hard-earned cash to come up here after all, looking to learn a bit more about the elements of style – and once they've hit those buttons, boom. Straight into the algorithm. If the numbers ever drop too low; it pings the system, the system notifies management; and management shift you off by close of play. Sometimes there's a little get-together. Sometimes there isn't.

The punters can rate you an Icon/Trendsetter/Too cool for school/Cool as a cucumber/Adequate/Dull or, worst of all – Tasteless.

For the last few months, I've consistently been Cool as a cucumber. But cucumbers aren't leaders. And that's where I need to improve. To help get me in the zone, I've stopped eating cucumbers.

'Tuna cucumber sandwich?' Eddie thrusts something brown and sloppy looking in front of my face and waves it around. It's been three days and he's still only in his boxers.

I shake my head, no. I am working on a new kind of stare. It's one I think might just bump me up into the Trendsetter category, where I can really start to show my style and leadership qualities. To make the stare work, I have to think particularly hard about what André Gide was trying to say about freedom and empowerment in the face of moralistic and puritanical constraints. I let my gaze fall somewhere off in the distance, and make my shoulders look more angular.

Eddie takes a bite of the sandwich he'd been offering and studies me for a moment. 'Woah,' he says, flecks of tuna fish flying from his mouth. 'Nice look.'

I receive the compliment without even an increased heartbeat. Because I do not give a fuck about anything. I feel nothing. And it feels great.

***

For a week, things start looking up.

For starters, I receive no new messages from Cassie about Shaun's allergies. He just has little lungs right now and the doctors have told us they're all scratched up. We know it's the house – it doesn't take a genius to do the equation that bad landlords, leaking pipes, entrenched damp, and children's lungs don't mix. And when you add in repeated, mismanaged pandemics and a healthcare system sold off and worn out by the folks at the top, well – there you have all the elements needed for scratched up little lungs.

It costs Cassie 10 credits to send a direct message to me here, which you don't need me telling you is too many credits. So she only sends a message when things are bad.

But, no message means things aren't bad at all! In fact, they might even be great. How am I to tell otherwise? And not only is there no news on the allergies front; I can also tell them I'm in a prime position for the promotion we need to get out of that house and shifted out somewhere more stylish. Or I could, if we could afford the credits.

I just need to stop thinking about Shaun's little lungs and keep on giving zero fucks. I might not be able to sing like Zoe. But perhaps I don't need to. If I can just get my new stare right, this new look could take care of everything.

There was a time when all this came totally naturally. That was when there were massed crowds outside the glass of our enclosure each day, when the flashes of cameras never ceased, when our faces and elaborate poses lit up social media, traded through the ether from one hot young influencer to the next. Those were the days when beautiful women would take their tops off and press their breasts against the glass, and gloriously chiselled men would pull their pants down to reveal how well-endowed they were. Each of these impossibly beautiful people before us vying for our attention – and we would look straight on past them all, perhaps rolling our toothpicks from one side of our mouths to the other with a gentle curl of our tongues.

In those days I had a new stare for every day of the week. Monday's was funky. Tuesday's was Avant Garde. Wednesday's was punk. Thursday's was minimalist. Friday's – of course – was casual. Saturday's was hipster. Sunday's was existential. And every day, through it all, staring right past the breasts and dicks and through all the flashing lights, the beat of my heart perfectly calm as I heard them yelling, "Jesus Christ would you look at his eyes. He doesn't give a fuck!"

These days, the no fucks giving takes work. It takes time, and it takes effort. It takes energy to tune out what could be almost at first a background noise of some whining insect nearby that starts way, way down beneath your skin, a whirring, sometimes in the pit of your stomach and sometimes in your chest, or caught in your throat, or else pulsating and vibrating right behind your eyes. But if you can master it. If you can truly make it outside of yourself. *That* is when you reach the zone. The zone of zero fucks-giving, with total and absolute absence of even the most atomically miniscule fucks, where not even through the most advanced computations of quantum physics could you uncover the merest possibility of any fuck being present in any place or in any time. It is devoid of emotion, positive or negative. It is infinitely neutral. Utterly and incontrovertibly indifferent. It is the Swiss delegation at a UN debate after taking enough Xanax to knock out an elephant. It is a holy, ethereal plain of absolute chill. It is my Everest.

That's why I'm so pleased I don't give a fuck about how much impact my new stare seems to be having.

***

After days with no punters, a couple of lonely folks with big guts showing under their tank tops waddle up to the glass. They peer in, captivated at first by Zoe, who is creating some explosive, paint-splattered artwork over a small canvas in the centre of our shared area. Then the one with a lonely-housewife look spots Eddie, lying on a chaise lounge eating a packet of tortilla crisps. Here's when things could've really gone south; but it is at this moment the lonely househusband spots me. His jaw drops. He nudges his wife, who lets out an excited little squeal and reaches into her flowery handbag for a camera.

'Do you see that,' the husband says. 'Now *that* is how I need to be. Contemplative, but suave. Assertive with my opinions. That's right, isn't it?'

'Yes, I think so,' says the wife. 'Should we ask them, do you think?' she gestures towards us.

'Well, indeed, uh, yes. Certainly. Rightio. Let's do that,' he says. He clears his throat and knocks politely on the glass of our enclosure. 'Excuse me?'

Zoe continues making her latest piece of art. She is painting style. Which is what she tends to do when not singing style, or writing it, or wearing it, or eating it or running it or fucking it. To make love with Zoe is to feel as though you have been brought to orgasm by Warhol, Mercury, Elvis, Simone, Hepburn, Kelly, Monroe and all the rest simultaneously.

'Wowee,' the man lets out an impressed whistle at this obvious cold shoulder. 'They really don't give a hoot, do they? No sir!'

'Ask them again," the woman says. 'Remember. Be assertive. It's like The Mantra says: think positive; be positive. Don't take no for an answer.'

'You're right. Gosh I love it when you quote The Mantra,' he knocks on the glass again. 'I say, ahem. You there. With the paint? Or perhaps you, over there, with those – yes, you're looking right at me I think, very nice. Very good! Would you mind – awfully – just, you know, giving us a few pointers? Pointers on how to be like you? Love your style! Iconic!'

Iconic. My heart-rate increases. I force it down.

'You won't get anything out of them,' Eddie shouts over towards the lonely folks with their guts and eagerness.

Their heads snap back as though surprised to remember his existence.

'Oh, hello there,' the man says, cautiously. 'Are you – are you part of all this then?'

'Part of this?' Eddie says. 'I'm an OG! Taught these guys everything they know.'

This is only partly true.

'Oh,' the man says. 'Is that so?'

'It certainly is, man,' you can almost see the old muscle memory creaking back into gear. As he says 'man', Eddie raises his hand up to his head and makes to flick his shades down in a smooth, practiced motion. The sort of trick he perfected years ago. The trouble is, his shades are nowhere near him. Flustered, he looks around, shifts his weight and reaches under his seat. But no dice. Or shades, for that matter.

'Well, in that case,' the househusband says. 'Maybe you could give us some pointers? While we've got you?'

'Shoot, hombre!' says Eddie.

'So, say I wanted to get noticed at work,' the man says. 'What's the way I might go about doing that. Is it something I should do? Something I should say? Should I tell people to peace out more?'

'It's not what you say, it's the way you say it, man,' Eddie says.

'Wowee, that's great. Gee whizz ain't that just great. Sally, Sally, are you taking notes of this? Where's your notepad. We gotta be taking notes of this.'

Sally begins hurriedly fussing about in her husband's large backpack and eventually pulls out a frayed orange notebook and a pencil with one of those fuzzy stationery toppers with googly eyes.

'And what about things we should be doing,' the man asks. 'Should we be watching more French films? Should we begin taking hardcore drugs?'

'The problem,' Eddie says, 'is when you ask – rather than just do.'

'Ask him about the sex,' the wife says.

'Okay, okay,' the man shushes at her. 'Apologies if this may seem indelicate. But, well, with all of y'all living here together, and being as, well, stylish, and attractive and all. Do you ever, you know, have intimate relations or suchlike?'

'Sometimes, sometimes,' Eddie nods. The husband lets out an excited snort then tries to compose himself.

'Even, um – even you? I mean, do you get involved with – all that?' the man stumbles over his words, which hang in the air like a fart.

Eventually, Eddie says, 'why wouldn't I?'

'Now, now, I didn't mean it like that, now.'

'Be assertive, Lloyd,' his wife hisses at him. 'Remember The Mantra.'

'How else would you mean it, *Lloyd*?' Eddie raises his voice.

Raising your voice is a big fat No-No when it comes to not giving a fuck about anything. Eddie should know better.

'Remember The Mantra!' the wife hisses again.

'Well, well. Actually, Perhaps I did mean it like that,' the husband almost seems shocked by his own words. 'Perhaps I meant that, to look at you – and I know this will sound, difficult – but to look at you, sir, you wouldn't think that anyone would want to do any sex with you at all.'

'Not one bit of sex with you at all,' the wife reiterates.

'Well *Gee-Whizz* guys!' Eddie is properly yelling now. There is not even a trace of cool cucumber about this. 'If it isn't waddle-duck Lloyd and big bloater Sally. The fuckleheads from whichever county still lets you marry your cousin, come up here to pay their credits and poke and tease some hard-working Eddie-'

'Eddie?' the husband says. 'Is that your name? Eddie? Write that down, Sally, write it down.'

'I'm writing it down, Lloyd, I am writing it down.'

'That's going right in the review.'

'Right in the review is where it's going.'

'Oh sure,' Eddie is standing now, rising from the large indent he has made on the padding of the furniture. 'Write a review, see if I care. My family has been through worse than a little review. You know, we were wearing Keffiyeh's before Louis Vuitton was selling them for 700 a pop. But we made folks like you think they were hip. Because you always wanna be like us; but you don't wanna admit that you actually like folks like us. That's why some folks wearing those *expensive* Keffiyeh's came to our house and burned it down with my grandma still inside. You know, she got turned into human soup by how hot it got? When the recovery team eventually dug their way in, there wasn't even any human bones down there – just a pool of liquified human, squelching around their boots. So, what's a little bad review to me? Write it all you want! It'll take more than a review to make human soup out of me I can tell you now.'

Eddie carries on like this for a long time, brandishing a fist in the air and screaming until Sally and Lloyd have disappeared down the hill and out of sight.

And this whole time, I've just been staring.

'Did you see those guys?' Eddie asks us. He wants us to join in. But to join in I'd have to give a fuck.

'It's like they were lost in negative space,' Zoe tells him. She has a kind of faraway edge to her eyes that she gets when her instinct to take a hipster-devil's advocate view of the world takes over. 'Two souls like Sisyphus, trying to find style. Trying to get that boulder to the top of their mountain. It was almost beautiful.'

'You think everything is beautiful,' Eddie says. 'Back me up here, man, c'mon.' He looks at me. His eyes are big and wet. When Shaun had his first attack, Eddie was the one who covered for me the weeks I had to stay in my separate area. He gave all the tips he earned those days to me, telling me it was nothing; and not to give a fuck about it. When the landlord wouldn't fix the dehumidifier, it was Eddie who organised the whip-round down at the Existentialist's Café and got everyone to chip in so we could afford a new one, then acted like it wasn't even worthy of acknowledgment – that was how few fucks should be given about it. Now he's a man who gives far too many fucks about far too many things.

What would a leader do in this situation? I think to myself. A leader would role model. That's what. A true leader shows others how it's done.

Eddie stands there in front of me with his big wet Eddie eyes. And I stare right through him.

***

We get our ratings that evening. Our consoles make delighted little digital noises to alert us, and we each get up and head over to check them out. I take care to do this neither too quickly nor too slowly. They're just ratings, after all. Sure, they could be the thing that gets me that promotion; or they could be the thing that gets me fired. But whatever, right? That's the attitude.

I boot up my console. After so long with no visitors, the system takes a while to wake up. When it does, I see not just one; but two green arrows. I watch as the descriptor "Cool as a cucumber" transforms into "Trendsetter".

A double rise is almost unheard of. Sally and Lloyd must have both rated me as Iconic and given some excellent qualitative feedback.

But I don't smile.

I barely even think about it.

I can't remember the last time I was a Trendsetter; but it is definitely the kind of grade that could help get someone a promotion, especially someone with leadership qualities.

We roll back into our shared living area. I yawn, scratch the back of my neck and start rolling a joint. Zoe starts pushing diamond studs into the cuffs of her leather jacket. Eddie sort of just sits, shoulders a bit hunched, staring at the floor.

I'm cool with the silence. I barely even notice it. When Zoe clears her throat and asks about our ratings, I couldn't care less.

'Trendsetter for me,' I tell her, shrugging.

She nods her head. 'Nice work, man.' The flush to my cheeks hardly registers.

'How about you, man?' Zoe asks Eddie.

He almost whispers it. 'Tasteless.'

Zoe and I shoot one another a look. That's a long time for Eddie to be sitting in the Tasteless zone. His overall algorithm rating must be near rock bottom. All the credit he earned back in the days when he was an Icon must have almost all been spent.

'Hey, don't sweat it, man,' Zoe tells him. 'Things'll pick up. You're an Icon – we all know it.'

Eddie lifts his head up, turns, and smiles at her. 'Thanks, Zoe, you've always been a good one.'

We hardly ever call each other by our real names. Not even being able to muster a 'dude' or 'pal' or 'mate' – things must be more rough for Eddie than I realised.

'Quit being like that, man,' Zoe urges. 'No need for that attitude! You're one bad character, remember? A real dangerous artist. When was the last time you even danced?'

'Danced?' Eddie blinks. There's a smile there, somewhere. His eyes cast about, searching. 'Zoe...'

'Yeah, man,' Zoe is saying. 'You know what I'm saying. You know what it's time for.'

She walks across to her music collection and starts flicking through records. When Eddie sees this, he stands and starts making the universal gesture with his hands telling her to cut it out.

'No, Zoe, no, c'mon, man. I'm really not in the mood for any Seamonkeys of Zarathustra.'

'This ain't the time for that shit, man!' Zoe is getting properly into this, now. Her hips are moving to a beat that hasn't even started. 'Aha!' she pulls a record out and holds it aloft. 'Now this. This is what I'm talking about.'

She slides over to the music station and pops the record in. She stands with both feet planted firmly apart and points the remote control at the speakers, turning the volume way up. Then she hits play and the sexiest sax I have heard growls out from the amp. I'm staring at Eddie, who has this light, mystified grin that's spreading across his face as he realises the exact song – it's one of Al's old favourites that he would play to get us all up on our feet at the Speakeasy all that time ago. Eddie's realising it just as I'm realising it – just as the drums start to come in and the honky tonk piano starts plonking its way into the groove; right before Ella's voice comes through the mix of it all – pure heaven, singing the elements of style more purely than I have ever heard them sung. Eddie is grooving, leaning his head right back and popping his chest while the rest of his limbs move like they're half liquid in perfect rhythm. Meanwhile Zoe is pure, straight ecstasy, eyes closed, hands and fingers twirling slowly around themselves. And without realising it I am on my feet with them both, feet sliding, fingers clicking, nerve-endings dropping. Listening to the whole beating world, enveloping us in immense, milky way-soft energy.

The songs blurred together, the tracks flowing one after the other into themselves until at last we came to one of the slow sultry ballads and I sat down on a chair, giddy from it all and a smile I could not shake. I watched Zoe and Eddie inch closer together, and Zoe slowly reached out her arms and held them across Eddie's shoulders, her fingers linked behind his neck, and his hands, slowly, reaching out and placing them on her hips and drawing her close to him, sinking his head down so that they were dancing with their foreheads touching. And after the chorus Eddie shifted his head again, and raised his hands from her waist, so that his head was resting against her chest and shoulder, and his hands were gripping her back. They stopped their gentle swaying, and soon, the only movement came from the heaving of Eddie's back as he sobbed. These big, thick, heavy sobs. And Zoe cradled his head and held him against her. And like that they remained until the music ended, and we were left in our shared living area, with nothing but the faded crackle fuzz of the record skipping over itself at the end of its time.

***

The next morning, we are greeted with a veritable throng of people outside our enclosure. But they aren't adoring fans. They aren't lonely househusbands or bored office desk jockeys. They aren't punters at all; they're management.

You can tell they're management because they all wear suits and give a fuck about absolutely everything.

The last time I saw management like this was when they closed Graceland.

I try to clear my mind. I angle my shoulders, and start staring.

I hear Zoe come in. I don't look at her but I can *feel* her standing there a moment longer than usual, taking in the sight of all this management.

Then Eddie joins us.

'There he is!' One of the suits near the front yells out. 'The man of the moment! A true legend! Everybody, please give a round of applause for one of our original style icons – Eddie!'

The gathered suits all burst into a sustained round of applause that lasts exactly thirteen seconds.

'Eddie, don't be shy. Don't be shy now. Come on and step forward. There's a good chap. We all know, don't we, that there comes a time, for each one of us, when we must recognise it is time for a change. A new phase in our lives. You may even have seen this documented on your screens from time to time – you know the shows I'm talking about, with the certain people from South America or Asia – or perhaps it is Africa, one of those – they gracefully recognise when they can no longer be of use to their tribe, and stand up, sometimes donning a beautiful headdress, and depart, often in the glorious dying light of sunset, never to be seen again; and actually in fact to die, alone, in a mountain or out in some marsh or somewhere remote and difficult to get to. So dignified. So pure. So much style, I'm sure you'll all agree. And just like these stylish tribes, it is time for us to recognise that it is time for one of our own number to depart.

So today, we must say good-bye to Eddie. Eddie, we are all so very sorry and sad to see you go. Unfortunately, we do not have a fancy headdress for you to wear – headdresses are expensive you'll understand – but we can all imagine you gracefully donning one right now, can't we, everyone? So please, Eddie, do take your metaphorical headdress along with the remainder of your belongings and ensure you are off the premises within the next thirty minutes.'

'Oh lord,' says Eddie. 'Let this not be real. Please let this not be happening. This can't be happening.'

But it is happening. This is the end of Eddie. We don't even have the opportunity to speak to him. Zoe and I have to stay in the zone for the whole thing. It's company policy.

Someone from management hands Eddie a large bin bag that he uses to go and collect his things.

'It's been an honour', says Eddie, trying not to burn any bridges. But he says it too desperately and we can all see the way he says it, hear it in his tone; there's nothing stylish about this departure. Perhaps with a really stylish departure they might have kept him in mind if things pick up again. But with a departure like Eddie's just then – there's no chance.

We all stand and the suits part in order to let him shuffle his way out of the enclosure and down the path towards the exit. Then the suit's attention falls briefly to me and Zoe.

'Now you two right here,' the first suit is saying. 'Don't think that just because we've come down here to send dear Eddie off, doesn't mean we haven't got our eyes on the pair of you. Let this be a shake up – a restructuring – no, a re-energising! Yes, a re-energising of your whole, ensemble. Because this organisation was built on team work, and energy. And we want lots of that from all our many employees. That's you guys, here on the frontline. We are counting on you! And we are always looking for stylish new leaders who have a bit of something about them, so–'

Suddenly, Zoe screams. She roars: 'Fuck. This!'

She spins around and charges out of our shared living space and into her own room.

I don't blink. I am not thinking about Eddie. I am not thinking about Zoe. I'm not thinking about Shaun, or bad landlords, or our no money. I am on my Everest. And I just keep staring.

'Look at this here,' the first suit says. 'Utterly exemplary. Now *this* is style. What are their ratings – Trendsetter and Icon? Did you hear the way she screamed? So passionate. So real. And see this one here – there's absolutely no fucks being given whatsoever. We need more of this. Yes. Much more. Very good, very good.'

***

That evening, I get back into my separate area and find a new message on my staff console. It's from Cassie.

'Hey, you,' the message reads. 'Things not good with Shaun. Any word on that promotion?'

I don't have the credits to write back.

The thing I feel most with Shaun is that I know he already gives too many fucks. How could he not? With his lungs and the situation at home and with me not being around.

When I was a kid, I spent entire afternoons hanging upside down from a tree, seeing how long it would take before my vision turned red and blurry. I'd lie on the grass with one hand blocking the sunlight from my eyes and sit by quiet streams and just *listen*.

But that's the thing about kids I guess, the no fucks giving comes more naturally. Or, at least, it should be.

Even with Shaun, there are times when I've been home that I've seen him really lose it. Usually it's when he's outside with the neighbour's dog – this ridiculous mop of an animal. And you see him rolling around with it, all laughter and kinetic energy. And it's like all the fucks in his life have just dissolved into the aether, evaporated.

It is a very, very long time since I was a kid.

WRITTEN IN STONE,
WRITTEN IN BONE

STEPHANIE BRETHERTON

She is made of the mother, of this she has no doubt, why then does the earth beneath her feet seem determined to destroy her?

Why has the sun hidden his face, denying her warmth and light? Why has he shrouded all she once loved?

Why has the ash from some heavenly fire smothered the water, stopped its flow and turned it into something beyond comprehension? Something hard, cold and unyielding.

Questions are useless. There is no one who can or will answer. There is only one foot placed in front of another. She treads on through a bitter wind, the child at her back sleeping now, exhausted from wailing out its hunger. But this is no place to stop. Her limbs complain as they push through the filthy snow, but she must reach the safety of higher ground. She must find some shelter, somewhere to make a fire.

Somewhere to dream. A new vision is needed to guide her on. And from higher ground she can choose the best route, the easiest terrain. A way forward through the expanse of grey snow, a way toward clear running water.

She is called by an inner song to glance upwards.

A hawk circles overhead. So. There must be prey here, even if small. She will search the ground beneath its flight, she will sniff out any signals from the soil and set some traps. But first, eyes closed, hand on heart, she places a prayer on the wings of the solitary bird above. A blessing to soar skyward. Even in the dark of a day with no sun, the heart must remember its own light. Otherwise, why keep walking? But walk she must. Walk, crawl, run, swim, seek, hunt, walk some more.

The cave was unexpected and could so easily have been missed. As she works her flint over the scant kindling, she makes a vocal offering to the feathered guide who had led her here. She begins a humming chant of gratitude that she hopes will also encourage a flame. The spark that sets her hopes alight may have come from within or without, it does not matter, but she thanks the hawk once more for the fat little rat that will roast when the fire is high.

It will be warm here soon. The tunnel through which she belly crawled, knees leaving skin upon stone, will keep the wind away from this cavern. The cavern she had sensed in the stillness, the cavern she had known she would find. But that narrow opening also keeps this hollow curve as dark as charcoal, and she works now only on faith and through the habit of her hands. The fire she sets will be the only sheltering warmth mother and daughter have known for far too long.

The child is awake but calm, knowing that comfort will come. Her mother also draws from the knowing of her soul, this is the gift of her bloodline, a line that surely must live on? Flames lick and snap at the roughly gathered roots and begin their shadow dance with the rock. These walls, she can see clearly in the firelight now, are made of the precious red rock. This is good. Good for making marks upon, good for chipping pieces away to mark her own skin and that of the child. Protection from so many hazards, symbols that call in her spirits, a salve against all the tiny creatures that bite and sting and suck.

None live here now (so few live anywhere) but once this place had been both honoured and cherished. She sees it in the simple pattern of crossed lines that have been etched and left by another above her head. Marks that say, *here*. Here is safe, here is good, here we have loved and cared for one another.

She learned to make her own story on the walls of a different cave. One where she and the child had suffered sharply and yet recovered well from a sickness like nothing she had experienced. The lightness in her head afterwards, and something about the strange carcass that she has stumbled upon there, something beyond recognition, had compelled her to do what she had often dreamed of doing but had never before dared.

There had been no other to tell her whether this was right or wrong, only what she could test as true within her own heart, like breath blowing through a bone.

She pulls a particular flint from her belt. One found so far behind them now, near a cliff of startling white. She had worked it well, this treasure. Worked gently to preserve the curling creature caught within its stony tomb, made the grip of the flint easy and good and perfect for the shape of her hand, made its blade sharp enough to carve many more blades. This place, this sacred place, is where its thinnest, sharpest edge will do its finest work.

She alone carries the story of her family, of her tribe. And she can do nothing but carry it onwards to the refuge, to the people she believes *must* emerge from dream and into living flesh. Sometime. Somewhere.

If neither she nor the child survives then the marks she will add to those already gracing these walls would rebuke the great mother for ending her bloodline but... yes, they would also thank the mother for lending her a body that was able tell another, any other, in whatever seasons hence, that once the world knew life and light, and perhaps one day there would be light and life again.

(*This story is set in the world of* The Children of Sarah, *a series of novels exploring what it is to be human – and the connections between ancient and modern, science and the sacred. The first book,* Bone Lines, *will be re-issued by Breakthrough Books, along with a new follow-up novel,* The Fire in Their Eyes, *in early 2025)*

About The Authors

Zena Barrie is a festival producer, writer and spoken word performer from Manchester. Her debut novel *Your Friend Forever* was published in 2021 and described as "a beautiful book about hope and perseverance" by Robin Ince. Her book of short stories, *Two Similar Looking Men With Umbilical Hernias* is due to be published in 2025.

Mark Bowsher is a proudly dyspraxic writer and filmmaker from Kent. His short story *The Hunger Wall* was published in the Fish Publishing Anthology 2023. His debut novel, YA fantasy *The Boy Who Stole Time*, was first published in 2018 and will be re-issued by Breakthrough Books in October 2024 alongside a new book in the Myrthali series, *The Dream-Peddler's Parade*. Mark has made three award-winning short films and 14 documentaries for Dan Snow's History Hit. He lives in Bristol and enjoys board games, travelling the world, swimming and long walks where he can conjure up exciting new adventures. Website: www.rabbitislandpro.co.uk Twitter: @markbowsherfilm

Stephanie Bretherton is an author and copywriter with a passion for the power of words, nature and science. A lifelong nomad and storyteller (in one medium or another) she now lives on a cliff in far west Cornwall. Her well-received, Kindle-bestselling novel *Bone Lines* will be followed by

The Fire in Their Eyes, book two in The Children of Sarah series in 2025. Short stories have been published in *Sunshine Superhighway* from Jay Henge and *Taking Liberties* and *Order and Chaos* both from Breakthrough Books. Website: www.stephaniebretherton.com

Jamie Chipperfield is a full-time carer currently living in Cornwall. This anthology is his third time in print, Jamie has stories in *Taking Liberties* and *Order and Chaos.* He is currently working on various writing projects as well as developing his interest in photography and design. Twitter: @jchipperfield3

Sue Clark feels she's found her true calling as a writer of contemporary comic fiction, after a varied career as a BBC comedy scriptwriter, journalist, copywriter, editor and PR. Her second comic fiction, *A Novel Solution,* was published in March 2024. Her debut, *Note to Boy,* came out in 2020. Her third is still a twinkle in her eye. Website: www.sueclarkauthor.com X, formerly Twitter: @sueclarkauthor

Jason Cobley is a semi-retired teacher with high blood pressure and a few books to his name. This includes an array of comics, the pastoral WW1 novel *A Hundred Years to Arras,* ghost story collection *Calendar of Ghosts,* and *The Rock Bled Black,* set against a backdrop of the Tonypandy Riots. He lives in Warwickshire. Website: jmcobley.wordpress.com

Stevyn Colgan is an artist, musician, speaker, lecturer and author of ten books. He was, for a decade, one of the primary writers of the BBC TV show 'QI' and was on the writing team that won the Rose D'Or for Radio 4's 'The Museum of Curiosity'. Stevyn is also co-host of the literary podcast 'We'd Like a Word'. Stevyn's highly popular and creatively eclectic YouTube channel, Colganology, can be found here: youtube.com/@colganology

Samuel Dodson is an award-winning writer and editor based in London, UK. He is the founder of creative collective, Nothing in the Rulebook. His first book, *Philosophers' Dogs*, was published by Unbound in 2021. Website: www.samuel-dodson.com Twitter: @instantidealism

Elena Kaufman is a Canadian writer, actor, and teacher living in Germany. She has an MA in Drama from Toronto and an MSt in Creative Writing from Oxford. Her plays have been showcased at festivals in Winnipeg, Stockholm, Paris, Vancouver, and Hamburg. Short fiction has been published in literary journals in Canada and the United States, and her anthology, *Love Bites and other stories*, was published by Unbound. *Residents of Room 12.01*, her latest collection of speculative and ghost stories, is looking for a publisher. She is a member of The Writer's Room in Hamburg where she lives with her physicist husband, twin boys, and a shaggy dog.

A.B. Kyazze is an author and photographer who worked for humanitarian organisations around the world before settling in London. She has published many short stories and three novels: *Into the Mouth of the Lion* (2021); *Ahead of the Shadows* (2022) and, writing as Amelia Kyazze, *The Café on Manor Lane* (2024). Her writing has been longlisted for the Mslexia Women's First Novel Prize in 2017, and for the Virginia Women's Writing Prize from Aurora Metro publishers. She also runs creative writing workshops exploring the senses, and is a trustee of the Oxford Centre for Fantasy, a creative writing charity. Get in touch via Instagram at @abk_writing or through her website.

Pete Langman is a cricketer, editor, musician, and writer (though not necessarily in that order). Following an unstellar career as a professional guitarist, he acquired a PhD and a diagnosis of Parkinson's Disease as consolation prizes. Since then, he has lectured at several universities, published *Slender Threads: A Young Person's Guide to Parkinson's Disease* (2013), *The Country House Cricketer* (2014), *Killing Beauties* (2020), and, most recently, *Spycraft: Tricks and Tools of the Dangerous Trade, from Elizabeth I to the Restoration* (2024), written with his partner, Professor Nadine Akkerman. His re-produced 1995 solo album *Dancing With Architects* (with special guest performances from a whole boxful of fabulous musicians) will be released in September 2024.

Virginia Moffatt has written two novels *Echo Hall* (Unbound) and *The Wave* (Harper One More Chapter) and a flash fiction collection *Rapture and What Comes After* (Gumbo Press). She is currently working on a couple of new novels and a novella and has stories in *Taking Liberties* and *Order and Chaos*. She lives in Dorset with her husband Chris.

Ivy Ngeow was born and raised in Johor Bahru, Malaysia. She holds an MA in Writing from Middlesex University, where she won the 2005 Middlesex University Literary Press Prize out of almost 1500 entrants worldwide. Her debut, *Cry of the Flying Rhino* (2017), was awarded the International Proverse Prize in Hong Kong. Her novels include *Heart of Glass* (2018), *Overboard* (2020) and *White Crane Strikes* (2022). She is commissioning editor of the *Asian Anthology New Writing* series. *The American Boyfriend* was longlisted for the Avon x Mushens Entertainment Prize for Commercial Fiction Writers of Colour 2022 and the winner of Singapore Book Awards 2024 for Best Marketing Campaign. She lives in London.

Penny Pepper is an award-winning author, poet, and disabled activist whose stories explore the disability narrative through provocation, humour and wisdom. Her memoir, *First in The World Somewhere*, was published in

2017; her poetry collection, *Come Home Alive*, in 2019. Her stories feature in *Hemingway Shorts* anthology 2021, Lumpen and Mslexia, and she's a columnist for news magazine Byline Times. She's currently working on a novel, *The Widow of Rock-o-Nore* – a tale of ghosts, disability, love and darkness. She lives in Hastings with her cat, Pixie.

After 37 years facilitating the construction of social housing in the UK, **Eamon Somers** returned (2023) to his native Ireland. Included in previous Breakthrough anthologies, his stories have also appeared in Chroma, Tees Valley Writer, and Automatic Pilot. The Journal of Truth and Consequence (University of Phoenix) nominated Fear of Landing for a Pushcart Prize. His debut novel *Dolly Considine's Hotel*, set in Dublin, was published in 2021. An LGBTQ+ activist, his story Poor Little Nat featured in Quare Fellas published by Basement Press in Ireland, and provided the inspiration for his forthcoming novel, The Man Who Gave It Away. Website: eamonsomers.com

Nicole Swengley is a London-based, freelance journalist who has written for the Financial Times, the Telegraph, The Times and Wall Street Journal amongst many other publications. Her short stories have featured in women's magazines, the Breakthrough anthology *Order and Chaos*, and a crime anthology from Pavilion. Her debut novel, *The Portrait Girl* will be published by Breakthrough Books in October 2024.

Damon L. Wakes has been writing one story a day every July since 2012, making for over 4000 at the time of writing and possibly quite a lot more by the unknowable future time in which you are reading this. He is also the author of *Ten Little Astronauts* – a sci-fi reimagining of Agatha Christie's *And Then There Were None* – and *Face of Glass*, a prehistoric fantasy novel. His other work tends towards the experimental, ranging from virtual reality games to procedurally generated religious texts, and occasionally involves wiring fresh bananas into other people's computers.

Wiskey is an artist (see *A storm in Heaven and Hell* which graces the cover of *Elemental*), writer, film maker, storyteller and philosopher. Currently working on five books in five different genres, he has published poetry (*Ecstatic Fire* 2009) and a traditional wonder tale (*Icsius* 2022) with Old Lady Press, and short stories (*In Other Words* 2021) with Unbound and (*It's About Time* 2022) with The Healing Press. His key interest is sacred art, which one of his documentary films is exploring, and which his vast painting project *Metanoia* endeavours to be. He lives in London with none of his 24 godchildren. www.wiskey.art

Acknowledgements

Writing is both agony and ecstasy (and a lot of procrastinating, nail-biting and imposter syndroming). Publishing is all of the above with uncountable hours of admin instead of the procrastinating. But the joy of a collective is the gentle pressure of all the other hands at your back, thus, there are always too many people to thank. Firstly, gratitude to all the authors included here, not only for their wonderful stories but for their collaborative efforts and skills in shaping the overall content.

Special thanks must go to J B Wiskey, the immensely talented artist who has kindly given us permission to use his stunning painting *A Storm in Heaven and Hell* to create our cover, and the collective's own mascot, Jamie Chipperfield, not only for invaluable support, but for working up said cover design and the interior typesetting. Thanks also to Stephanie Bretherton for all the sleeves-rolled, head-down, brow-furrowed, blue-aired, cheer-leading blood-sweat-and-tears. (She loves it really, hyphens, parenthesis, ellipses... and all. And if you notice any "quirky" punctuation in this book, it's a style thing, ok?)

Also From Breakthrough Books

Taking Liberties, a highly regarded anthology of short stories on the theme of freedom.

"A cornucopia of delights. From the very first story I was struck by the skill and literary nature of the writing. Many have plots that would translate brilliantly into television dramas or films, with so much packed into them. An intelligent, carefully crafted and rewarding collection with something for every reader." — Linda Hill, Linda's Book Bag

"Although very different, the stories are all extremely well written and elicit a plethora of emotions in the reader. All of human life is here, and you will be delighted by the variety of approaches the writers have taken." — Julie Morris, A Little Book Problem

"A brilliant collection of short stories and slices of life that will stay with you, and leave you wanting more!" — Ste Sharp, author

In Truth, Madness, a novel by TV reporter, Imran Khan, about a war correspondent on a journey of awakening that drives him to the edge of sanity.

"A Neil Gaiman style spectacular set across the ancient and present day Middle East."— Laury Silvers, author of The Sufi Mysteries Quartet

"A beautifully written, magical tale of mental health and international news." — Dareen Abughaida, principal anchor for Al Jazeera English

"Unusual. Intriguing... I couldn't put it down." — Barbara Mainville, book critic.

"Funny, clever, relatable and deeply moving." — Horia El Hadad, documentary maker

Order & Chaos, Breakthrough's second highly regarded short story anthology

"A perfect short story book at bedtime" — Jenny Nisbet

"An imaginative, diverse, thought-provoking and often brilliant anthology. Excellent reading. Wow, there's some good writing in these pages." — Stephen Sheppard

"My first read from Breakthrough Books and it certainly did not disappoint. Brilliant stories from cover to cover. Thought-provoking, insightful, funny, paranormal, amusing and shocking, Order and Chaos has everything. It's full to the brim with great writing, it's entertaining, moving, chilling and interesting." — David Brockway, book blogger

"A brilliant and eclectic mix... this collection is a must read for any short story fan who wants to experience something different and give themselves something to think about." — The Book Elf

Before You Go

We hope you enjoyed our stories as much as we enjoyed writing them. They exist through dedication, passion and love. Reviews help encourage readers to give this book a chance and you'll be helping the community to discover and support new writing. It can take less than a minute and just a line or two is enough. Please leave us a review wherever you bought this book or wherever you prefer. A big thank you in advance on behalf of everyone in the Breakthrough Books collective.

For all the latest news, find us on Facebook, or follow us on Instagram, X, BlueSky or Threads.

www.ingramcontent.com/pod-product-compliance
Lightning Source LLC
Chambersburg PA
CBHW031306120726
47906CB00003B/908